PRAISE FOR *SERAPHIM AND THE DUST PLAGUE*

Kraszewski delivers, with his unique combination of humor and hyperbole, a compelling and entertaining story that speaks as much about a literal plague as it does a more subtle one bending the hearts and minds of modern man. When the dust settles, we are left reflecting on the grander truths about life, God, and free will, and at least considering the manner in which we relate to our neighbor, or greet the stranger walking by us on the street, or simply live our day-to-day lives, in what seems like trivial moments, in our own beautiful towns.

—BENJAMIN FOREMAN, business owner and optometrist

Nostalgic.
Utopic.
Be transported to another world, perhaps another time.
Be invited to see in a different way.
To have challenged your reason.
To believe.
To love.

—FR. CHASE HASENOEHRL, pastor at Saint Augustine's Vandal Catholic and PhD candidate at Oxford

What a remarkable tale that left me thinking and rethinking long after I put it down! Kraszewski expertly weaves together vivid small-town imagery, thoroughly human characters, and the threat of a nearly apocalyptic Dust Plague to enchant the reader. His quirky prose had me smiling, and at times, laughing aloud. In peculiar and unexpected ways, this story explores what it means to be human, what we become in the face of death, and what might just be needed to catch us off guard and shock us into the truth.

—AMY MCNELLY, M. Div, CEO, Palouse Care Network

Seraphim and the Dust Plague is a parable that moves with remarkable celerity to its heavy hitting conclusion. Pithy and engaging to the last line, this is an immensely enjoyable read for an evening that you planned to waste away on Netflix . . . but why eat mincemeat when you can have Filet Mignon?

—DR. CECILY "ALWAYS-LATE-TO-THE-PARTY" KRESLINS

SERAPHIM AND THE DUST PLAGUE

Seraphim AND THE Dust Plague

a novella

BY
GRACJAN KRASZEWSKI

AROUCA PRESS

ISBN: 978-1-990685-94-1

Arouca Press
PO Box 55003
Bridgeport PO
Waterloo, ON N2J 0A5
Canada
www.aroucapress.com
Send inquiries to info@aroucapress.com

PART ONE

I.

It is by all accounts a most beautiful
town.
Entering from the sky one glides
down
slowly over a perennial
brown-green of hills so soft, so rolling, so tucked one
on top of the other it's tempting to think I could be
too, nestled under one of them as if enveloped by a
thick blanket, snug, soon on to a deep and restful sleep.
If you're lucky enough to be gliding
down when the sun
is sinking, consider yourself very lucky. Out the window fields of lentils, barley, dry peas and wheat; and
look, right there, look, you're low
enough
to make out the details, affixed to a red barn a rusty
basketball hoop, two brothers wearing matching
crimson-candy apple Cougs sweatshirts, and so far
it's been
three three-pointers made in a row,
now a fourth,
they high five,
and although now you're gone, now they're too far
away, who knows?, maybe they won't miss a shot the
rest of the evening, hitting threes until the sky turns
purple and their mother calls them to dinner by way
of a ringing cowbell.

Feet crunching on pebbly gravel up to the front door, shoes off, leave those shoes outside, socks pulled off alternatively balancing on one foot while the opposite hand pulls off the sweaty former clingy "stuff," that "material," the socks off then rolled up then thrown carelessly into the corner. Bare feet so cool,

so refreshing,

perhaps plainly

cold on the interior tile. C'mon now, boys, we're waiting, hurry up, it's been ready for a while. No, no, no, first, haha, but of course, off with the two of you!; hurry, make sure you use the good soap and really get that dirt under the nails.

Heaping plates of stew plus lentils;
thick, foamy beer for Dad;
Dad then getting refilled by
Mom because, boy, that stew is really something;
each brother eating, eating heartily;

see: they play, they eat, they grow.

Dad cleans up after dinner while Mom runs a bath for the boys, a bubble bath, and she draws it hot enough that each one can take his time because brothers and parents of brothers know brothers want and need the treatment(s) to be wholly and always equal, and there's no need to add warm water because it's been just right all the while.

Dad forsook the dishwasher in favor of doing the dishes by hand and anyone who's really spent a good quarter-hour on the scrub, soak, steel wool pad pressing of a considerably thorough dishwashing knows how good that feels on the hands. They prune slowly, then all of a sudden, the hands. The skin on them, the hands, draws tighter, a rough callous or two sheds an upper layer of skin. You keep exfoliating those fingers that palm and it's not long before you understand this is pretty close to what it's all about. That maybe the introduction of the dishwasher machine into the mid-century American home was more of a punishment, a deprivation of the simplest pleasures of daily life, rather than time saving convenience.

"Mom, can Dad come in and read to us?"

And so he does.

And then they go off to bed, post story, post bed-time prayers and sing your ABCs silently while you brush your teeth.

And then maybe, finally, the married couple can sit down and have some time to themselves.

II.

You land, you disembark, the plane itself small enough to mistake for a toy, the airport befitting the cozy theme.

One runway,

one transit lounge,

two vending machines

that sell nostalgia-soaked treats like *Ms. May's Chunky Chocolate Chip Cookies, Wowzers' Waffle Snaps* and an orange-soda drink called *Atomic Fizz.*

Atomic Fizz, why not, and it really pairs well with Ms. May, you got two bags of those, I mean they were 90 cents each, not even one buck, take that *Dollar Tree,* and it's all in a nice stride, an easy flow here, for you landed and a real, literal ten minutes later, snack stop included, were turning the steering wheel left or right as you exited the parking lot on your way home.

Home? Where is home?

I don't know.

Who are you?

That would be my first question.

Where do you live?

I assume not Spokane for Spokane has its own, larger airport, one with name brand snacks. Lewiston too. If we deductively reason down that *most likely* not Colfax, not Uniontown, not Colton, not Palouse—although these do qualify, proximately speaking—we're left with a left turn towards a large, state university and a right turn, this way across a border, an elegant state line so crisp let's call it a frontier, towards a large, state university.

Right turn it is.

And remember that it is, by all accounts, even popular acclaim, moreso professional journalistic stamps of approval via panegyrical articles employing florid prose and all the right descriptives in glossy magazines, a most beautiful

town.

Much of the credit must be attributed to the local power couple team Mr. and Mrs. Craigmore. Lucy Craigmore, Mayor, recently re-elected by an outstanding 77% of the vote and Dave Craigmore, her husband, local land oligarch, if you will, who made no small fortune in the California real estate game in snazzy, stuffed to the rafters rich Caramel-by-the-Sea and then brought that capital with him,

here.

He made money, bona fide cash, earning him a page near middle of the magazine, bottom right-hand corner, inset mini feature in *Forbes.* The story said his favorite professional sports team is the New York Giants. It said he likes to listen to jazz and read Jane

Austen to "relax." He listed hobbies including fly fishing, hiking, making my own granola, and volunteering at the animal shelter.

Something people love about Dave is that he used to be a regular at Clint Eastwood's Thursday night poker games. Yes, he owns just about half the buildings in

town,

and he loves this

town,

our

town,

and gives a lot to keep it looking good, properly maintained, but tie him down for a cup of coffee at B___'s or OW___'s or even quaint M___'s affixed to the Catholic Center on Deakin, well, he'll spin that yarn until it frays then splits then disintegrates. Tell us Dave, did Clint really wrestle an authentic razorback once? Clint drank how many ____? Clint actually ___ at _____when he was supposed to be promoting _____ on the red carpet? Dave, please be serious, did Clint really claim that ____ happened after ___ and ____ went to ____ with ____? No way,

Dave,

stop,

Dave,

for the love of humanity!

Lucy dotes on her husband, loves him in that *my man that's my man* type old fashioned way, but as Mayor Lucy she sometimes wishes he'd promote the city activities as much as he does Clint Eastwood.

It is a beautiful

town.

Things are going good, maybe threatening to boom into some kind of roaring 20s minus Black Tuesday

and the depression. The Main Street farmer's market has tripled in size, expanded up to the corner of Rosauers and Gas Station Bermuda Triangle dispensaries number 6,
8
and 2.

They still make those extra doughy, gingerbread reduction, all the throwaway parts patched back together slab-smack that icing on top plus maybe a raisin, bars;

Rosauers.

How do you do it, meaning, how do you eat it? You pour a glass of milk or get someone to bring you a glass of milk and you place that glass next to a plate or the box, *the* not *a* box, because if the box it's the main container holding all of these and intent has been declared. A plate, maybe one or two bars but the box means business, you mean business, you're about to get down to it and getting to the point here means a slow dismemberment of each and every bar by way of a soft plucking motion, thumb and index finger doing all the work, as you pull away, depart slash remove or disassociate the new piece from the original bar, and gently place it into your mouth followed by a sip of milk; again, again, again, again . . . again. The contact liminality of milk on gingerbread mediated by your tongue, taste buds, and saliva is sublime.

Boise State University is considering opening up a local branch campus called BSU-Panhandle and for no other reason than respect and a hoped slice of the pie, to be where the action, the star power, the very green glint of the Gem state happens to be at the present moment. And these people know green glint and pie slices for no one can doubt the

blue turf had quite the run. From legends of ducks/
crashing into imaginary lakes/
to the very real Kellen Moore go route caught by Titus Young/
on a foggy Friday night midnight WAC feature/
(while C. P., the head honcho, looked on.)/
It was good while it lasted even if all good things must come to an end.

A house in the Fort Russell district sold last year for 2.3 million.

Many homeowners have hot tubs and they take hot tubs at the same time of day, late evening, so as to have neighborhood block parties each person in his or her own hot water. They play music very loud, publicly, in this

town,

but it is always, without fail, classical music, Mozart roughly thirty percent of the time.

A brisk walk in the university arboretum on a cold autumn morning when it's foggy but not so much you can't see the moose, hard to beat, that.

Brisk walk, what about running (?),
what about you and your spouse, your soulmate, out on a run (?) in this one and same place and it's snowy as in it has snowed and there's about two inches maybe three on the ground so today cranberry bog wader style boots not tennis shoes are in order and thus affixed to your sock covered feet and you're on that good glide pace today because two things that overcome the awareness of sub-optimal conditions are love and good conversation and having them both means, on mornings like these, having it all.

The

town

was ranked #8 on Top 10 best places to raise a family in America. The Co-op is the only grocery in the country to feature a selection of Mongolian cheeses and Black Sea wine. A local artist also named Dave, not the Mayor's husband, got his work showcased at the Met in NYC last fall. And to think, the local paper wrote in the aftermath, he's been here all along.

But so where have we been (?), they asked.

St. Mary's School added 9 through 12 five years ago and last year the varsity girls Volleyball team took state. Team titles, athletic crowns, you ask? Just don't ask if the partying on the one and same Main Street was an adjective tornado equal parts grand, rowdy, boisterous, intense, overbearing, pugnacious, joyful, cheerful, unintelligible, and inscrutably mirthful when the University's football team won the FCS national championship. Don't ask if the head coach was at the head of the parade his head doused see drenched in apple fritter juice marmalade.

Good times.

II.

Maybe, in the present moment, now, things are not so beautiful in other places, and otherwise, in America. But are people here supposed to care that for the first time since 1815 America could go to war against Great Britain;

or, that Canada recently signed an economic and military "special friendship" treaty with the Chinese;

or, that the national debt last month broke the quadrillion mark after a few years hovering in the 990 trillion-dollar range?

Just last week Maine's *Portland Press Herald* ran the following headline:

Mysterious Dust Bowl like Dust storm, Hybrid Geological Event with "Bacteriological Pathogenic Effect," Baffles Scientists and the Medical Community in Nova Scotia.

Probably not;
interest, caring, here, the people in this
town.

But if this is true, can you blame them? What a bumbling, rambling headline that was, is, and you think people here read Maine newspapers? I doubt many of them know what's happening in Portland, Oregon.

That the article details said best bets are that it might just be unprecedented, this, the dust storm plus bacteriological pathogen—so you're saying an airborne virus propelled in wind funnels, you're saying go look at photos of that, the Dust Bowl, but now that dust falling doesn't just coat your farm, your mouth, your dreams, it's an infection agent, a bio-warfare waves of madness maybe—even these details might not make people who believe they don't need to care, care. A strict quarantine in Halifax, residents told not to go outside, close windows, tape them shut if you have to, just stay indoors, keep your head down, dust, dust everywhere. Kudos to the *Press Herald.* They did slap down an easy to remember name for the event, the thing, whatever it is.

"The Dust Plague."

Back here,
it is a beautiful
town.

Lucy loves the expanded farmer's market and especially the throngs of people who patronize it. She really likes that they bring their money too, fat wads of cash, many of them. These throngs, thick like locust, stroll the main drag, they buy, buy, buy, buy, buy, buy, buy,

buy

buy

buy [1]

sample sometimes take large bites eating, eating this, that, oh, you really gotta try, okay, look, just one bite, one bite, bite, bite, I bit my tongue, bite, bite

bite,

bite,

bite

now chomp, ooh, that's good. When the weather's good it's grand, and sometimes she'll stroll down to stroll on through herself, admiring, what is to her, not that she'd admit this openly, a life's work, a masterpiece, a teleological drive starting with the end in mind the ends justifying the means the means being good old fashioned hard work, easy smiles, a soft pat on the back, deftly placed words of encouragement, substantial dollops of business acumen (thanks, Dave!), and just the slightest tweak-fine tuning concerning marketing, promotional postures, well timed interviews, hype, buzz, and an already sterling reputation set in perpetual motion so as to always be preceding itself. Quite simply, the end goal is Lucy's desire for this to be the best

town

in the history of

1 Buy, buy, buy, shop, purchase, buy, cardswipe, debt, second mortage, buy, take stuff you bought last week to the thriftshop, at the thriftshop we buy then donate again, again, buy, I'm so sad actually, does anybody care? Buy, buy....

towns.

And it's not just all the positive *additions* to the

town

Lucy has overseen that matter. She's good at subtraction too. Yes, it takes talent and foresight and good management to build a place well. But you have to pull up some weeds too, have to be good at pruning, trimming the fat. Problem number one in this regard were the activities gone common, bi if not tri weekly, at a mid-point on Main Street, truly at the center of the beloved farmer's market, called Friendship Square. Betraying its name, Friendship Square had become center stage for all kinds of public spats between the various rival factions in

town.

A protest of Israel drew counter protestors denouncing Iran. Much like in the actual Middle East, the two sides accomplished little other than yelling insults at one another but here, in this

town,

right out in the open air, for all to see. It was the same for every type and stripe of cause that, for whatever reason, found itself pooling around and about Friendship Square; believers vs. atheists, climate alarmists vs. climate hoaxers,

the political left vs. the political right,

the right being yelled at by the extreme right who were being cheered on by the

alt left while the extreme right

attacked the right only to change course, the

alt left did, when the

alt-extreme left started attacking them.

And all of this, to Lucy's dismay, on the grounds of so-called Friendship Square.

Lucy took action.

Lucy deracinated some weeds.

Issuing an official proclamation that Friendship Square was to be renamed "Philadelphia Court," for mere friendship had proven woefully inadequate, what was needed was "a commitment to universal brotherly love," she banned, under the penalty of a domino trigger of cascading fines and citations, any type of speech, demonstration, rally and/or intellectual and/or propagandic showing of whatever sort. When certain unhappy parties protested at the next city council meeting that this was a clear violation of multiple First Amendment rights, not to mention the dictionary definition of unfriendly and anti-fraternal, Lucy, calmly but with a quiet determination, explained, now, by inference, by, *hey, read between the lines here,* for she would never, of course, never plain state something like this, no, but it was obvious to all what she meant when she made known that some of the people at this meeting had submitted certain building proposals and permit applications and other assorted paperwork that she herself, personally, was going to have to approve and, *well, gentlemen, wouldn't it be just such a shame if those documents somehow got lost?*

Lucy won.

Philadelphia Court became a model of silent stability, a monument to void, to absence, to a lack of noise, of commotion, of people in the still bustling on farmer's market days city center but amidst them a hole, a space, a separation island of non-noise, of contrast, especially, and it was all going just so great, so properly excellent in this, here, this beautiful

town,

until the day he showed up.

III.

One man. Dressed in a brown zip up sweater, bluish gray pants, white tennis shoes, his hair neatly combed to the side, he even wore glasses, an uncommon touch for those in the homeless community. He was slightly built while also seemingly fit. He looked to be about 170 pounds and under six feet tall; five foot nine or ten inches and maybe one hundred and sixty eight point four pounds and affixed with or beset by, in a good way ("blessed with"?), reserves if not a reservoir of hidden strength.

5'9 168 but he deadlifts 515, for reps.

5'9 168 but his lower body strength is good enough to dunk, from the foul line, or from a two foot stance onto an eleven foot hoop.

5'9 168 but he fights men in cages for money in front of crowds.

5'9 168 but his body fat is single digits, his abs a V-8 engine of a six pack, and so it's not surprising he runs a sub 5 minute mile and sub 4.5 40;

and so on.[2]

For five days now he was all day and every day and then into the night, overnight, found sitting, then laying down, sleeping, on Philadelphia Court. Five days was fine enough for this stunt, this whatever this was, Lucy thought, she now growing a bit concerned, but if he was still there tomorrow, during the Farmer's market, something would have to be done. The

town

had not had a case of homelessness in more than a decade, pre-dating Lucy's tenure, and she was not about to allow standards to slip on her watch.

2 and so forth.

But he was there the next day. And the full market flowed on by and around him as though he was not, as if he didn't even exist. But a promise was a promise, even if just made to herself, and so Lucy sent a few policemen to speak with the man, right as the booths were being taken down and the last fruit baskets piled away into freezers for long journeys home.

"Well," she says, when the policemen return to issue their report, "is he gone?"

"Um," one of the officers says, "I don't. I don't know, ma'am."

"What do you mean you don't know? You don't know, you don't know what?"

"We spoke with him," the other officer says. "And we passed along your directives clearly and firmly. That it is illegal to partake of any type of demonstration in Philadelphia Court and that furthermore camping out, squatting, prolonged loitering, is expressly forbidden there and throughout the city."

"Then what's the problem?" Lucy says, "Did you order him to leave?"

"Yes."

"I don't understand."

"We ordered him to leave, ma'am. But he explained that he could not leave. He said he had come here, and was staying here, because of matters of the gravest importance."

Lucy scoffs and stepping back almost trips over a small pile of books next to her desk. "This is your interpretation of the law, Officer," saying his last name with a clear touch of derision. For the second policeman she skips over titles altogether, angrily pitter patter repeating his last name three times then saying, "and you're going along with this! You're supporting this type of 'law enforcement.' How very modern, I see, just how lovely and compassionate, and well, woke. A police force that asks the offender if he wants to suffer the penalty for his crimes. And what do you know, you know what, no, no I think I would like not to be charged, yes, I think I'll just carry on my merry—

"We fined him," the first officer says. "We told him to leave. He did not leave. We proceeded to inform him that refusal to leave would mean a citation. He said that was okay, that he understood. We issued the citation and told him we would be back the next day, and the following day, and that each day he refused to comply with the city ordinance he would be fined. He . . . he thanked us, he shook each of our hands, told us he understood. Then we left."

"Get out of my office," Lucy says. "Get out."

She almost trips on the books a second time and that would have taken the cake, that would have been just what she needed now, the cherry on top, her clean and orderly

town

slowly slipping into anarchy, a rogue and renegade police force aiding delinquent revolutionaries and then she, had this happened, sporting some kind of awful bruise on her cheek or forehead from hitting the desk on the way down. She picks up the pile of books and smacks them down on the table. People say petulant outbursts of anger only exacerbate the bad feelings of a worked-up situation. What idiots, she thinks, picking up the pile and this time really slapping it down on the desk. It sounds good, reverberating like a large, wet fish crashing into aluminum siding. It feels good.

What she had not yet picked up off the floor, nor noticed, was that day's *New York Times,* formerly covered over by the pile of books. Once a story moves from the *Portland Press Herald* to the *New York Times* it becomes generally understood that things are afoot, things are getting serious. And on the front page no less:

DUST PLAGUE CROSSES OUR BORDER. HEALTH OFFICIALS UNANIMOUS ONLY IN UNCERTAINTY. BURLINGTON, VT, SYRACUSE, NY, UNDER QUARANTINE. THESE CITIES, AND MANY MORE, SUBMEREGED IN DARKNESS. TENS OF THOUSANDS FEARED DEAD. CDC TELLS MID-ATLANTIC REGION AND GREATER NYC METRO REGION TO MAKE PREPERATIONS NOW. "WE DON'T KNOW MUCH AT THE MOMENT," CDC DIRECTOR SAYS. "WE DO KNOW IT'S MOVING SOUTHEAST, MOVING FAST, AND THAT IT IS DEADLY."

Lucy sits down.

Lucy closes her eyes.

Lucy slumps back in her seat.

Lucy sees the words "Dust Plague" in her mind's eye. Materializing there against the pure black of shut eyes, eyes shut being rubbed, thoroughly.

Lucy then imagines the Dust Plague as a fine helixed number-letter code reading (and why these she would not be able to say. They were meaningless, that at least, and at last, was some certainty amidst a highly uncertain and ever changing situation) "XoxY2xp."

XoxY2xp—the Dust Plague in its foundational script—was lines upon lines of the extrapolated out numbers and letters in gray font.

Lucy fell asleep, in her chair, fixating on this code in her mind, on her mind, (but) on to what next?

```
X x x x x x x x x x x 0 0 0 0 0 0 0 0 0 0 x x x x x x
x x x x x x x x Y Y Y Y Y Y Y Y Y Y Y Y 2 2 2 2 2 2 2
2 2 2 2 2 2 x x x x x x x x x x x x x x p p p p p p p
X x x x x x x x x x x 0 0 0 0 0 0 0 0 0 0 x x x x x x
x x x x x x x x Y Y Y Y Y Y Y Y Y Y Y Y 2 2 2 2 2 2 2
2 2 2 2 2 2 x x x x x x x x x x x x x x p p p p p p p
X x x x x x x x x x x 0 0 0 0 0 0 0 0 0 0 x x x x x x
x x x x x x x x Y Y Y Y Y Y Y Y Y Y Y Y 2 2 2 2 2 2 2
2 2 2 2 2 2 x x x x x x x x x x x x x x p p p p p p p
X x x x x x x x x x x 0 0 0 0 0 0 0 0 0 0 x x x x x x
x x x x x x x x Y Y Y Y Y Y Y Y Y Y Y Y 2 2 2 2 2 2 2
2 2 2 2 2 2 x x x x x x x x x x x x x x p p p p p p p
```

X x x x x x x x x x x 0 0 0 0 0 0 0 0 0 0 x x x x x x
x x x x x x x x Y Y Y Y Y Y Y Y Y Y Y Y 2 2 2 2 2 2 2
2 2 2 2 2 2 x x x x x x x x x x x x x x p p p p p p p
X x x x x x x x x x x 0 0 0 0 0 0 0 0 0 0 x x x x x x
x x x x x x x x Y Y Y Y Y Y Y Y Y Y Y Y 2 2 2 2 2 2 2
2 2 2 2 2 2 x x x x x x x x x x x x x x p p p p p p p
X x x x x x x x x x x 0 0 0 0 0 0 0 0 0 0 x x x x x x
x x x x x x x x Y Y Y Y Y Y Y Y Y Y Y Y 2 2 2 2 2 2 2
2 2 2 2 2 2 x x x x x x x x x x x x x x p p p p p p p
X x x x x x x x x x x 0 0 0 0 0 0 0 0 0 0 x x x x x x
x x x x x x x x Y Y Y Y Y Y Y Y Y Y Y Y 2 2 2 2 2 2 2
2 2 2 2 2 2 x x x x x x x x x x x x x x p p p p p p p
X x x x x x x x x x x 0 0 0 0 0 0 0 0 0 0 x x x x x x
x x x x x x x x Y Y Y Y Y Y Y Y Y Y Y Y 2 2 2 2 2 2 2
2 2 2 2 2 2 x x x x x x x x x x x x x x p p p p p p p
X x x x x x x x x x x 0 0 0 0 0 0 0 0 0 0 x x x x x x
x x x x x x x x Y Y Y Y Y Y Y Y Y Y Y Y 2 2 2 2 2 2 2
2 2 2 2 2 2 x x x x x x x x x x x x x x p p p p p p p
X x x x x x x x x x x 0 0 0 0 0 0 0 0 0 0 x x x x x x
x x x x x x x x Y Y Y Y Y Y Y Y Y Y Y Y 2 2 2 2 2 2 2
2 2 2 2 2 2 x x x x x x x x x x x x x x p p p p p p p
X x x x x x x x x x x 0 0 0 0 0 0 0 0 0 0 x x x x x x
x x x x x x x x Y Y Y Y Y Y Y Y Y Y Y Y 2 2 2 2 2 2 2
2 2 2 2 2 2 x x x x x x x x x x x x x x p p p p p p p
X x x x x x x x x x x 0 0 0 0 0 0 0 0 0 0 x x x x x x
x x x x x x x x Y Y Y Y Y Y Y Y Y Y Y Y 2 2 2 2 2 2 2
2 2 2 2 2 2 x x x x x x x x x x x x x x p p p p p p p
X x x x x x x x x x x 0 0 0 0 0 0 0 0 0 0 x x x x x x
x x x x x x x x Y Y Y Y Y Y Y Y Y Y Y Y 2 2 2 2 2 2 2
2 2 2 2 2 2 x x x x x x x x x x x x x x p p p p p p p
X x x x x x x x x x x 0 0 0 0 0 0 0 0 0 0 x x x x x x
x x x x x x x x Y Y Y Y Y Y Y Y Y Y Y Y 2 2 2 2 2 2 2
2 2 2 2 2 2 x x x x x x x x x x x x x x p p p p p p p
X x x x x x x x x x x 0 0 0 0 0 0 0 0 0 0 x x x x x x
x x x x x x x x Y Y Y Y Y Y Y Y Y Y Y Y 2 2 2 2 2 2 2
2 2 2 2 2 2 x x x x x x x x x x x x x x p p p p p p p
X x x x x x x x x x x 0 0 0 0 0 0 0 0 0 0 x x x x x x
x x x x x x x x Y Y Y Y Y Y Y Y Y Y Y Y 2 2 2 2 2 2 2
2 2 2 2 2 2 x x x x x x x x x x x x x x p p p p p p p
X x x x x x x x x x x 0 0 0 0 0 0 0 0 0 0 x x x x x x

x x x x x x x x Y Y Y Y Y Y Y Y Y Y Y Y 2 2 2 2 2 2 2
2 2 2 2 2 2 x x x x x x x x x x x x x x p p p p p p p
X x x x x x x x x x x 0 0 0 0 0 0 0 0 0 0 x x x x x x
x x x x x x x x Y Y Y Y Y Y Y Y Y Y Y Y 2 2 2 2 2 2 2
2 2 2 2 2 2 x x x x x x x x x x x x x x p p p p p p p
X x x x x x x x x x x 0 0 0 0 0 0 0 0 0 0 x x x x x x
x x x x x x x x Y Y Y Y Y Y Y Y Y Y Y Y 2 2 2 2 2 2 2
2 2 2 2 2 2 x x x x x x x x x x x x x x p p p p p p p
X x x x x x x x x x x 0 0 0 0 0 0 0 0 0 0 x x x x x x
x x x x x x x x Y Y Y Y Y Y Y Y Y Y Y Y 2 2 2 2 2 2 2
2 2 2 2 2 2 x x x x x x x x x x x x x x p p p p p p p
X x x x x x x x x x x 0 0 0 0 0 0 0 0 0 0 x x x x x x
x x x x x x x x Y Y Y Y Y Y Y Y Y Y Y Y 2 2 2 2 2 2 2
2 2 2 2 2 2 x x x x x x x x x x x x x x p p p p p p p
X x x x x x x x x x x 0 0 0 0 0 0 0 0 0 0 x x x x x x
x x x x x x x x Y Y Y Y Y Y Y Y Y Y Y Y 2 2 2 2 2 2 2
2 2 2 2 2 2 x x x x x x x x x x x x x x p p p p p p p
X x x x x x x x x x x 0 0 0 0 0 0 0 0 0 0 x x x x x x
x x x x x x x x Y Y Y Y Y Y Y Y Y Y Y Y 2 2 2 2 2 2 2
2 2 2 2 2 2 x x x x x x x x x x x x x x p p p p p p p
X x x x x x x x x x x 0 0 0 0 0 0 0 0 0 0 x x x x x x
x x x x x x x x Y Y Y Y Y Y Y Y Y Y Y Y 2 2 2 2 2 2 2
2 2 2 2 2 2 x x x x x x x x x x x x x x p p p p p p p
X x x x x x x x x x x 0 0 0 0 0 0 0 0 0 0 x x x x x x
x x x x x x x x Y Y Y Y Y Y Y Y Y Y Y Y 2 2 2 2 2 2 2
2 2 2 2 2 2 x x x x x x x x x x x x x x p p p p p p p
X x x x x x x x x x x 0 0 0 0 0 0 0 0 0 0 x x x x x x
x x x x x x x x Y Y Y Y Y Y Y Y Y Y Y Y 2 2 2 2 2 2 2
2 2 2 2 2 2 x x x x x x x x x x x x x x p p p p p p p
X x x x x x x x x x x 0 0 0 0 0 0 0 0 0 0 x x x x x x
x x x x x x x x Y Y Y Y Y Y Y Y Y Y Y Y 2 2 2 2 2 2 2
2 2 2 2 2 2 x x x x x x x x x x x x x x p p p p p p p
X x x x x x x x x x x 0 0 0 0 0 0 0 0 0 0 x x x x x x
x x x x x x x x Y Y Y Y Y Y Y Y Y Y Y Y 2 2 2 2 2 2 2
2 2 2 2 2 2 x x x x x x x x x x x x x x p p p p p p p
X x x x x x x x x x x 0 0 0 0 0 0 0 0 0 0 x x x x x x
x x x x x x x x Y Y Y Y Y Y Y Y Y Y Y Y 2 2 2 2 2 2 2
2 2 2 2 2 2 x x x x x x x x x x x x x x p p p p p p p
X x x x x x x x x x x 0 0 0 0 0 0 0 0 0 0 x x x x x x
x x x x x x x x Y Y Y Y Y Y Y Y Y Y Y Y 2 2 2 2 2 2 2

2 2 2 2 2 2 x x x x x x x x x x x x x x p p p p p p p
X x x x x x x x x x x 0 0 0 0 0 0 0 0 0 0 x x x x x x
x x x x x x x x Y Y Y Y Y Y Y Y Y Y Y Y 2 2 2 2 2 2 2
2 2 2 2 2 2 x x x x x x x x x x x x x x p p p p p p p
X x x x x x x x x x x 0 0 0 0 0 0 0 0 0 0 x x x x x x
x x x x x x x x Y Y Y Y Y Y Y Y Y Y Y Y 2 2 2 2 2 2 2
2 2 2 2 2 2 x x x x x x x x x x x x x x p p p p p p p
X x x x x x x x x x x 0 0 0 0 0 0 0 0 0 0 x x x x x x
x x x x x x x x Y Y Y Y Y Y Y Y Y Y Y Y 2 2 2 2 2 2 2
2 2 2 2 2 2 x x x x x x x x x x x x x x p p p p p p p
X x x x x x x x x x x 0 0 0 0 0 0 0 0 0 0 x x x x x x
x x x x x x x x Y Y Y Y Y Y Y Y Y Y Y Y 2 2 2 2 2 2 2
2 2 2 2 2 2 x x x x x x x x x x x x x x p p p p p p p
X x x x x x x x x x x 0 0 0 0 0 0 0 0 0 0 x x x x x x
x x x x x x x x Y Y Y Y Y Y Y Y Y Y Y Y 2 2 2 2 2 2 2
2 2 2 2 2 2 x x x x x x x x x x x x x x p p p p p p p
X x x x x x x x x x x 0 0 0 0 0 0 0 0 0 0 x x x x x x
x x x x x x x x Y Y Y Y Y Y Y Y Y Y Y Y 2 2 2 2 2 2 2
2 2 2 2 2 2 x x x x x x x x x x x x x x p p p p p p p
X x x x x x x x x x x 0 0 0 0 0 0 0 0 0 0 x x x x x x
x x x x x x x x Y Y Y Y Y Y Y Y Y Y Y Y 2 2 2 2 2 2 2
2 2 2 2 2 2 x x x x x x x x x x x x x x p p p p p p p
X x x x x x x x x x x 0 0 0 0 0 0 0 0 0 0 x x x x x x
x x x x x x x x Y Y Y Y Y Y Y Y Y Y Y Y 2 2 2 2 2 2 2
2 2 2 2 2 2 x x x x x x x x x x x x x x p p p p p p p
X x x x x x x x x x x 0 0 0 0 0 0 0 0 0 0 x x x x x x
x x x x x x x x Y Y Y Y Y Y Y Y Y Y Y Y 2 2 2 2 2 2 2
2 2 2 2 2 2 x x x x x x x x x x x x x x p p p p p p p
X x x x x x x x x x x 0 0 0 0 0 0 0 0 0 0 x x x x x x
x x x x x x x x Y Y Y Y Y Y Y Y Y Y Y Y 2 2 2 2 2 2 2
2 2 2 2 2 2 x x x x x x x x x x x x x x p p p p p p p
X x x x x x x x x x x 0 0 0 0 0 0 0 0 0 0 x x x x x x
x x x x x x x x Y Y Y Y Y Y Y Y Y Y Y Y 2 2 2 2 2 2 2
2 2 2 2 2 2 x x x x x x x x x x x x x x p p p p p p p
X x x x x x x x x x x 0 0 0 0 0 0 0 0 0 0 x x x x x x
x x x x x x x x Y Y Y Y Y Y Y Y Y Y Y Y 2 2 2 2 2 2 2
2 2 2 2 2 2 x x x x x x x x x x x x x x p p p p p p p
X x x x x x x x x x x 0 0 0 0 0 0 0 0 0 0 x x x x x x
x x x x x x x x Y Y Y Y Y Y Y Y Y Y Y Y 2 2 2 2 2 2 2
2 2 2 2 2 2 x x x x x x x x x x x x x x p p p p p p p

IV.

Naturally, once the Dust Plague appeared on the front page of the *New York Times,* fear and fascination gripped the country. In only ten days since the man arrived in Philadelphia Court, and the officers talked to him, and then talked to Lucy, and then Lucy smacked her books on her desk in frustration, the situation here in

town

had gone full blown critical. The homeless situation, that is. Yes, yes, it was now confirmed that the Dust Plague had clipped on by[3] past New York and D. C.—and that was no small cause for celebration, the American president, when exiting his bio-contamination bunker openly thanked God for sparing the capital, and then went on to name God nine or ten times more in his speech, even approaching the very Old Testament exodus out of Egypt pharaoh precipice of beginning to, well it seemed like he was going there anyways, openly speculating if America was receiving a type of divine chastisement or something and perhaps we deserved it and perhaps it was time to look inward, all of us, even if just to metaphorically put on sackcloth and ash and . . . *wait, is that the sun, clear skies, repentance, um, folks, never mind all that,* he said in transition, coming fast

---

3
Xxxxxxxxxxx0000000000xxxxxxxxxxxxxYYYYYY
YYYYYY222222222222xxxxxxxxxxxxxppppppp
Xxxxxxxxxxx0000000000xxxxxxxxxxxxxYYYYYY
YYYYYY222222222222xxxxxxxxxxxxxppppppp
Xxxxxxxxxxx0000000000xxxxxxxxxxxxxYYYYYY
YYYYYY222222222222xxxxxxxxxxxxxppppppp
Xxxxxxxxxxx0000000000xxxxxxxxxxxxxYYYYYY
YYYYYY222222222222xxxxxxxxxxxxxppppppp

to his separation of Church and State senses.

Confirmed now, 10 days since, confirmed, that D. C. and New York and down the Atlantic Coast through
Virginia Beach unto
Cape Hatteras, and
Charleston, and
Savannah, all
the way towards the
Florida Keys and the
Gulf of Mexico had been spared.

Confirmed too, by way of a hazmat suit post-mortem picking through the rubble, that aforementioned Syracuse had been Carthage style salted to the earth by this thing.

X x x x x x x x x x x 0 0 0 0 0 0 0 0 0 0 x x x x x x
x x x x x x x x x Y Y Y Y Y Y Y Y Y Y Y 2 2 2 2 2 2 2
2 2 2 2 2 2 x x x x x x x x x x x x x x p p p p p p p
X x x x x x x x x x x 0 0 0 0 0 0 0 0 0 0 x x x x x x
x x x x x x x x x Y Y Y Y Y Y Y Y Y Y Y 2 2 2 2 2 2 2
2 2 2 2 2 2 x x x x x x x x x x x x x x p p p p p p p

About one hundred and fifty thousand call, rather had called, this home. "Everyone's dead, they're gone. They're gone, they're dead," the breathless report came over the phone. Two further questions went unanswered. The man had broken down into tremorous sobbing and had dropped the phone. A colleague picked it up, explained that this was in fact, unfortunately, the reality on the ground. No survivors were anywhere present. Tons of corpses lay about the

town.

They looked like they had suffered a Great War mustard gas attack. The dust appeared to eat through metal. The man explained he had watched a stop sign, covered in dust, get eaten way into nothingness—*annihilated* in the most precise definition of the word—as if by some acid within only a few hours.

Confirmed now, that the storm was heading next towards the Ohio Valley, Xxxxxxxxxxx000000 0000xxxxxxxxxxxxxxYYYYYYYYYYY22222 2222222xxxxxxxxxxxxxxppppppp

then on further west.

Chicago was already a ghost

town.

Lucy had more important things to worry about. In these latter ten days the man had not moved from Philadelphia Court, had been fined daily, was still wearing his brown zip up and blue-gray pants, but now, and just try to imagine the horror from Lucy's perspective, had attracted a mini following of sorts, other homeless people, and as of today there were seven squatters, all men, who had taken up residence. The cops were sent in again. Fines handed out, this time triple the amount, and, for the first time, threats of arrest and detainment made.

Five of these six new arrivals, unlike the original man, who, despite his apparent circumstances, was rather well kempt, were homeless like out of central casting: visibly drunk before noon, preferring a side shuffle staggering to walking, huge beards, eyes always asquint looking glued up, never fully open, saggy, their eyes, their pants, their general way of being and then the dirty baseball caps too, sometimes worn sideways almost falling off as if standard or reverse would be some kind of concession to society, untied shoes, one guy wearing one sock inside a shoe his other foot bare inside a shower sandal still wet always looking wet day after day; and there was singing and carrying on and it wasn't long before the crowds that so often filled the down-

town

to shop and sip coffee and push children in strollers were stopping and just kind of observing, studying, even, the growing collection of men, sitting, apparently doing nothing, unless that fortieth rendition of "99 bottles of beer on the wall," counts as something. And who is anyone to say that it does not (?), count.

Five of the six new guys unlike the original guy with the seventh and final guy the most extreme of them all. "I am Seraphim!" he would yell, periodically, and these were outbursts like a geyser at Yellowstone; sudden and sky high. These emanations were near apoplectic in their excitement and as varied as seemingly nonsensical.

"Down with the fixed price of 2% milk!"
"Cats and dogs and mice and
sunflowers and cake!"
"Kansas, Kansas, Kansas, good old
Kansas all the live long day!"

are expressions the man calling himself Seraphim yelled, a top a home-fashioned soap box platform, from his newfound home in Philadelphia Court. Seraphim wore blue faded jeans that were not quite long enough, didn't quite reach his perpetually untied, steel toe work boots. A tight fitting and prodigiously stained, the stains looking like coffee stains, tank top did its best to cover his ample midsection. And he wore a yellow Trucker's hat with a rather long message printed upon it in small font reading:

I'VE SUNG IN THE GREATEST CHOIR
IN THE WHOLE UNIVERSE.

Seraphim started entertaining passersby, especially

the kids, with his ability to burp out any song upon demand. "Mary had a little lamb" is the current favorite.

Lucy, as you can imagine, was just about beside herself. It had been more than two weeks now since first arrival, talking, fines, book slapping and what was bothering her most of all was that people here, not just this

town,

but the larger Palouse region, were starting to show a palpable open fear regarding the ongoing westward march Xxxxxxxxxxx000000000xxxxxxxxxx xxxxYYYYYYYYYYYY222222222222xxxxxxx xxxxxxxppppppp

of the Dust Plague.

Chicago, thank God the evacuations had been ordered and executed in timely fashion, had been Syracused, "acid eaten" down to the bone, the famous tourist spot The Bean in Millennium Park of particular note for one had to see the photos of what remained to believe your eyes. And when those winds came in off of Lake Michigan and drove the dust across Lakeshore drive and whipped the storm round and round throughout the city center as Amish women of old whipped butter by way of large wooden spoons plunging about thick, wooden barrels, churning,

churning,

churning, well,

perhaps it's better to stop there, out of respect.

The Dust Plague kept on marching[4], was supposedly now somewhere over Nebraska, poor Omaha, North

---

4
Xxxxxxxxxxx000000000xxxxxxxxxxxxxYYYYYY
YYYYYY222222222222xxxxxxxxxxxxxppppppp
Xxxxxxxxxxx000000000xxxxxxxxxxxxxYYYYYY

Platte you might be next, but Lucy, Lucy couldn't understand why people were so worked up about the possibility, the potentiality, not the guarantee, just the chance, that this storm might *hypothetically* arrive here, to this

town,

when they were already suffering a far more dangerous plague.

Business in the city center was down. People were disturbed. Never before had so many complaints come in to Lucy's office; that how was one to feel safe walking in down-

town

with *them* there; that how could a citizen possibly carry a coffee or an ice cream walking past Philadelphia Court when it might be stolen, ripped right from one's hands, at a moment's notice; that if Lucy didn't "take care of this now, immediately, *we,* the voters, *will take care of you and your political career at the polls.*"

One woman had been walking past Philadelphia Court holding organic, brown eggs, fresh from the Co-Op, the quality here truly top notch, alongside a glass cased matching quart of organic milk for which she had paid the pretty penny of $17.99, when Seraphim exploded skyward shouting,

"Tis the season to be jolly, jolly ranchers, jolly ranchers I promise you all!"

The surprised woman dropped it all, the eggs, the milk, smashing and crashing upon the concrete. She's now threatening to sue the city, and Lucy personally,

---

YYYYYY2222222222222xxxxxxxxxxxxxxppppppp
Xxxxxxxxxxx0000000000xxxxxxxxxxxxxxYYYYYY
YYYYYY2222222222222xxxxxxxxxxxxxxppppppp
Xxxxxxxxxxx0000000000xxxxxxxxxxxxxxYYYYYY
YYYYYY2222222222222xxxxxxxxxxxxxxppppppp

for one million dollars; for damages related to the lost produce and owing to the emotional distress suffered. She's going to go through with the lawsuit she has assured the Mayor unless she, Lucy, comes up with a "final solution to our problem."

Lucy decided to call in Dave. He's good with people, good at talking, allying with, then persuading. It's precisely these characteristics that made him such a formidable businessman. And so he went, walked down to Philadelphia Court. He asked the brown sweatered man if he'd care for a game of chess. *Certainly*, the man replied. Dave unfurled a green and white portable board from its brown sheath, opened the bag, dumped it all out onto the table. Dave even brought a chess clock because it's the little details that matter.

The other man won the first game in four moves; pawn to E-4. Queen to F-3. Bishop to C-4. Queen to F-7, this final move taking opposing pawn. Check mate. Both men laughed out loud. People claim to know all about this basic, simple, I mean you would have to be an idiot, have to have had a lobotomy to fall for *that.* Then they fall for that; it; four moves not a move more.

"Wanna play again?" Dave asks.

"Of course," the man says, flipping the board around so as to change sides.

Ten minutes in—and this time the game was hotly contested, each player having early on lost his queen, a bishop, and while Dave both his knights the man had stupidly sacrificed a rook, so it really was up for grabs at this point—Dave got down to business.

"So, if you don't mind me asking," Dave leads in, taking a pawn with a bishop before gently tapping the clock, "why are you doing this?"

"Excuse me?"

"This," Dave repeats, "is this a . . . a statement, a political statement? You know, some kind of... cause you're supporting?"

The man says nothing. He takes a pawn with a pawn then taps the clock.

"I'm just," Dave says, "I'm, curious, we're all curious. I don't mean to offend you. It's just that the Mayor has really, well, she really cares about the

town

the appearance of the

town.

And I gotta be honest—

"No offense taken," the man says, cutting him off.

Dave cannot believe his ears. "No offense." "No offense," he intones to himself, again and again, internally, silently, as he pretends to be deeply pondering his next move on the board. "No offense." *Oh, yes, I know this guy. Yes, that voice, that voice voicing that precise phrase. This is Mark Wilkins! Mark Wilkins,* still completely to himself, eyes down, now fiddling with a piece. The chess clock is ticking. It waits for no man. *Mark Wilkins, the former congressman, the representative of the next district next door. The—*

"Mark," Dave finally says, aloud. "Mark, why are you doing this?"

The man looks at him. "It's your move," he says, pointing to the clock.

"It's you, right? Mark Wilkins. It's, Mark Wilkins, it's, it's you."

"Are you going to move or not?" the man asks.

Dave moves a pawn. It's a pointless move, considering the state of the board at present.

"Yes," the man, now confirmed to be Mark Wilkins,

says. "Yes, it's me." He takes the pawn Dave just moved.

"Why are you doing this?" Dave says, once more. "What is this? Are you really, you know, down on your luck? Do you need money, are you, no, this is a, this is some kind of performance, an act, isn't it?"

"It's not a stunt," Wilkins replies.

Dave says nothing but does not stop staring at him.

"It's not a stunt," Wilkins says, again. "But I can't say anymore. I can't talk about anything else. Just no, it's not a stunt. Nothing to do with politics, nothing like that."

"Look," Dave says, having paused then pushed the chess clock to the side. His body language is textbook exasperation. "What am I supposed to tell my wife?"

Wilkins bursts out laughing. It's a beautiful laugh because it's authentic. He is neither snickering nor scoffing nor deflecting nor attempting to mock. He is laughing, laughing hard.

"I'm sorry," he finally says, clearing his throat. "I don't know. This has nothing to do with her."

"Nothing to do with her?" Dave says. "She's the mayor!"

Wilkins starts laughing again.

"You know," Dave says, "I could have you arrested. I really could. That's what she wants. You know, a lot of people want that, for your information. A lot of people. But, no, I said, no, I told her. Let me talk to him, talk some sense into him."

"Talk some sense into me?" Wilkins says. "I thought we were just two guys playing chess in the fresh air on a beautiful, sunny afternoon. Two people trying to salvage something of human custom, of friendships forged on the fly before that dust thing shows up here."

5

"One call," Dave says, extending his index finger. "One call is all it would take for me to have you and your whole . . . cohort, posse, arrested, one call!" The two of them look away briefly to look at Seraphim. He's changed his shirt but is still wearing his yellow

I'VE SUNG IN THE GREATEST CHOIR
IN THE WHOLE UNIVERSE

hat. He's doing some kind of workout that involves, at maximum speed completing seven push-ups, then seven crunches, then ten air squats and repeat, repeat, repeat and he's going, truly, full speed, and his form is properly ghastly, something like you couldn't do it with worse form if horrible form was what you were aiming at, if you were trying to employ bad form.

Wilkins now looks back at Dave. "Ah, you know how the saying goes. 'You would have no power over me where it not given to you from above.' One call, please, you think that's going to, what, 'break me?' I'm just sitting here, aren't I? Is sitting and sleeping in a public space illegal? No drugs, no drink, we're not too loud, I think. Tell your wife this: I'm not leaving because I cannot leave. No matter how many threats of arrest come my way, no matter how many of these I'm issued," pulling a crumpled up wad of citations from his pocket, "I cannot quit this space, as it were. I was asked if I would accept this mission and I had a choice, we always have a choice, and I said yes and here I am and here I am going to be. And that's it. Believe me, I wish I could tell you more so you could tell her more. I can't speak about it. I'm sorry."

5
Xxxxxxxxxxx00000000000xxxxxxxxxxxxxxYYYYYY
YYYYYY2222222222222xxxxxxxxxxxxxxppppppp

Dave gets up and leaves. How peculiar, he thinks. Yes, it's not strange or weird or baffling or confusing or annoying. It's peculiar.

V.

A stalemate of sorts set in regarding Wilkins + 6, on one side, and the other side consisting of Lucy and Dave and the city and the woman who had threatened to sue because of spilled milk, she, obviously, disregarding the wisdom that there's no use crying over it and, well, she had still not gone through with the lawsuit and so maybe she had been blustering and bluffing the whole time and speaking of things gone, but in the negative, things not gone, Wilkins and Seraphim and the other five men, they were not gone and nobody really knew what was going to happen with what the local newspaper had taken to calling

"Showdown in Philadelphia: PNW edition."

During this stalemate, the town appeared to return to a sense of pre-arrival normalcy, a position of tolerance, even. The homeless guys were there and so what? The farmer's market was still booming, it had never stopped booming, and that went a long way towards setting Lucy at ease. Maybe, just maybe, she thought, the seven men could render some service back to the community. *I mean*, she said to herself, *we haven't kicked them out, have not arrested them, we've even stopped fining them. What if they became a, some kind of like, a, an attraction during the market? Photobooth on Philadelphia Court with the Seven Dwarfs . . . ah, no*, she thought, *no, no, but something, something that can be marketed, yes, something to have them earn their keep, I'll keep thinking, I'll keep working on it*, she resolved.

Nobody was aware that the man in the brown zip up sweater, the blue gray slacks, Wilkins, was, in fact, former Congressman Mark Wilkins. Dave had kept that to himself. Why? Who knows? It was just, all, a very peculiar situation. And as for all the people on the street, did they not notice him? No, no because we don't really like to look at a homeless person, certainly not in the eyes. Your own father could be out on the street and there's a good chance you'd walk right past him. During one farmer's market two brothers, each wearing matching crimson-candy apple Cougs sweatshirts, one of them holding a basketball under his arm, offered Wilkins a twenty dollar bill given them by their grandmother, she of the opinion that charity not only starts at home but that the lessons about charity extending beyond the home begin at home too. He thanked the boys politely but told them he didn't want their money, didn't want any money from anyone.

That was the most peculiar thing of all: nobody knew what he wanted.

The plague kept moving westward[6], people kept frequenting the down-

town,

the men remained in the down-

town,

Lucy was pacified, at least partially, and life was progressing as life usually does; hundreds of hidden compromises, pushes, pulls, unseen side steps and the overall will to keep going, even with one's head down and the coat buttoned and zipped to the top. This because even though it was seemingly coming, there was good hope, so said the experts, that the

town

would be more like New York City and Washington D. C. than timely evacuated Chicago. Forget Syracuse, no chance of that.

6
Xxxxxxxxxxx000000000xxxxxxxxxxxxxYYYYYY
YYYYYY222222222222xxxxxxxxxxxxxppppppp
Xxxxxxxxxxx000000000xxxxxxxxxxxxxYYYYYY
YYYYYY222222222222xxxxxxxxxxxxxppppppp
Xxxxxxxxxxx000000000xxxxxxxxxxxxxYYYYYY
YYYYYY222222222222xxxxxxxxxxxxxppppppp

And then, it all changed.

People never understand this. They sit, dumbfounded, and ask, often aloud, how hijacked jets could have hit the twin towers on a morning where there was not a cloud in the striking blue sky. As if hijacked jets on an overcast day satisfies some nebulous, pseudological sense of rationality.

As if from overcast skies: we should have seen it coming.

The front page of the *New York Times* on September 11, 2001, and so mind you, this would have been delivered via a paperboy's well placed throw, shoulder launch to brownstone stoop thump, at five AM or six AM or maybe 6:30 in the morning, depending on the route, but, nonetheless, well before the first plane hit the North Tower at 8:46, this front page of the one and same *NYT* having been written and printed mere hours before/earlier than that (the paperboy's delivery; of course, the linear timestream obvious here), and it read, on the front page, in the bottom right-hand corner, on that fateful morning, coincidence of coincidences because a cold case warmed up today:

"Traced on Internet, Teacher is Charged in '71 Jet Hijacking."

And you read that, so many years after the fact, and you shake your head and mutter that we should have seen it coming.

They sit, dumfounded, and ask how the Japanese could have just decided to bomb Pearl Harbor and then gone through with it and in one real day of chronological history and then afterwards it was done, they had done it; ask how, I mean because all the polls told us, all the pundits swore it was true, that it was going to happen in favor of Mrs. ____hyphen____, that an American electorate chose the New York businessman over the former First Lady, ex-Secretary of State; ask how, even, even yes, even stupid, puerile, infantile questions like "but how did our team jump out to a 21-0 lead at halftime and then lose? How is that possible?" How did they lose after the quarterback threw a pick six and then the next series the running back fumbled and then the next play the other team scored on a double-reverse flea-flicker back to the QB and although at that time it was still 21-14 in favor of your team the momentum had shifted and made easy understanding of that same team, the opponent, going 5 for 5 in subsequent series, all touchdowns, to close it out 49-21;

how?

That's the how you're asking about,

really?

Possible is possible, always possible, owing to the reality of change and agents of change. And people just do not ponder this long enough. Terrorists, sneak attack pilots, voters, many of whom, the voters, would never admit they were going to vote for ____ but then did vote for ___ because they, like terrorists and sneak attack pilots and even all the amalgamated parts of the football experience, the players, the coaches, the referees, are agents of change capable, even when only possibly, of creating change, and sometimes they do, sometimes they make change happen. And things like whatever this Dust Plague is are certainly agents of change that can change like all changing things do, and when doing so cause changes and change, more generally and grandly speaking, to occur.

But it's about stopping to ponder this.

VI.

The Dust Plague was going to miss them, pass on to the south, yes, evacuate Boise, get Nevada on the horn get Nevada emptied, even the far reaches of that Loneliest Road in America U. S. 50, where nobody lives anyways, where you can't find two gas stations or two broken soda machines less than 200 miles apart, get everyone out, head West, wait, south, go really south, cross the border into Mexico if you have to, swim the Rio Grande southward, backward, dog paddle style, freestyle, breaststroke or butterfly, with or without floaties,

while or while not getting filmed by grama,
college girls by the pool smiling,
or not,
1950s prototype suburban husband dad and businessman grilling poolside barefoot on green well-watered grass,
or not,
shirt on or off,
shoes on or off,
look, whatever, man,
just get you and yours to safety there's no time to lose,

all this,
all that,
had changed,
because things do change

and now, the Dust Plague at present time down to seconds and milliseconds in its swirling, acid eating through metal through everything turbulent wind funnel churn over north central Wyoming

X x x x x x x x x x x 0 0 0 0 0 0 0 0 0 0 x x x x x x
x x x x x x x x Y Y Y Y Y Y Y Y Y Y Y Y 2 2 2 2 2 2 2
2 2 2 2 2 2 x x x x x x x x x x x x x x p p p p p p p
X x x x x x x x x x x 0 0 0 0 0 0 0 0 0 0 x x x x x x
x x x x x x x x Y Y Y Y Y Y Y Y Y Y Y Y 2 2 2 2 2 2 2
2 2 2 2 2 2 x x x x x x x x x x x x x x p p p p p p p
X x x x x x x x x x x 0 0 0 0 0 0 0 0 0 0 x x x x x x
x x x x x x x x Y Y Y Y Y Y Y Y Y Y Y Y 2 2 2 2 2 2 2
2 2 2 2 2 2 x x x x x x x x x x x x x x p p p p p p p
X x x x x x x x x x x 0 0 0 0 0 0 0 0 0 0 x x x x x x
x x x x x x x x Y Y Y Y Y Y Y Y Y Y Y Y 2 2 2 2 2 2 2
2 2 2 2 2 2 x x x x x x x x x x x x x x p p p p p p p

was going to crash into them, within days, maybe hours like 36 hours, a day and half, crash into them in a direct hit and yes, I'm sorry to report, that was the prognosticated consensus all around, we regret to say that it is going to be exactly like Syracuse,
maybe worse.

One moment the collective consciousness of the
town
was that the Dust Plague would pass them by therefore don't worry about the Dust Plague. Go back to fighting with your spouse, road raging someone at the next light, worrying about what color halter top goes best with purple jeans, yeah, I'm looking at you, buddy, you clown, use a turn signal next time, what you're

getting for dinner later, if you should bring your dog to a no dogs park because he'll be on a leash and no one will notice anyways, me?, me?, I'm to blame, me?, I had right of way, you imbecile, you absolute idiot, believe me, if I could get your license revoked I'd do it, asking at what point though is spaghetti too crunchy to call al dente, wondering why people will unfailingly first look at and fixate upon themselves in any photo even though they ostensibly know what they look like better than what anyone else looks like and so why keep obsessing on things old and known(?), and why postmodern life, or whatever this is, has become so plastically suffocating that the thought of a massive and all-out war where first the big bombs fall and then the survivors build trenches out of the rubble and eventually get to hand to hand combat worthy of the Punic Wars[7] when all the technology fails and rusts out seems desirable and soon exhilarating and why, is there some connection(?), and internet quick-searching how best to ice a swollen face because a road rage *light* incident escalated beyond those borders spilling over the sides and you took a swing and missed but he in hitting back connected and it just really plain old hurts now, and

if it's worth texting him back or not, I mean, why not(?), it's just a text.

One moment, don't worry.

The next moment, next moment like a split second later where the passing of time is not felt, it is just not felt, not comprehended, not taken in like passing through a door from snow outside to fire-heated warmth indoors, there and then you feel and

7 Or, alternatively, the Pacific Theater islands of the Second World War.

comprehend the transition as it's happening, no, here, one moment, next moment, the next moment is now, now we know, we know, all of us, individually and as a whole as we've all found out all at once and at once as in suddenly, it's coming for us, and soon, and so it was chaos;

everywhere.

Many people in the down-

town

dropped items in hand and started sprinting as if running from a tidal wave or some King Kong monster stomping in from the horizon. To their cars, reasonable, one might say, assuming they're thinking, ok, a day, day and half maybe two,

turn that key, key, key,
fill the tank, that tank, tank,
drive, drive, drive,
drive away.

Other people were actually standing in place, as if frozen, and screaming, loudly. One lady, she not screaming, sat down on a bench and started scanning for flights on her phone. If one sat down next to her they'd see she kept typing in Barcelona as point of origin, destination either Dehli or Tokyo, and she kept going back between those two, in terms of where to land, but always out of Barcelona, so she was not doing okay. One guy picked up a rock and threw it through a storefront's main window. Luckily, no one followed his cue. People were much too terrified to riot. He looked around a few times in that *what did I just do*? fashion before himself breaking into a sprint and disappearing down some side street.

Wilkins and the six other men were still in Philadelphia Court. Wilkins had been sitting, the usual of the past month plus, and maybe it had been two months now, who was counting?, sitting and seemingly doing nothing besides, but at least he was calm, placid like a high altitude, snow melt fed lake, his eyes, blue and clear like Flathead Lake at sunrise, yes, he looked calm because he was calm and as the world looked to be ending around and about him he got up, stooped briefly to tie his shoes, and started walking across

town.

He was going to see Lucy.

PART TWO

I.

"What do you want?" she asks him, standing behind her desk.

He didn't even bother to knock. He walked right through the front door. It was open. He's standing in the doorway now. Not that protocol or custom matters at this moment. There's no front desk reception, no staff, no "team." They're gone. Maybe the question is why is she, Lucy, still here?

"I need you to tell everyone not to leave the town,"

Wilkins says.

One sentence, and she recognizes his voice, just like Dave had. She sits down. "Mark Wilkins, it's been you, the whole time? You're the, the homeless-

"I need you to tell everyone: do not leave town"

he says again, now stepping fully into her office and sitting down himself. "They need to know this. Everyone. Tell them not to leave, please."

Lucy makes a start to speak but then shakes her head, side to side, twice. She lets out a chuckle.

"Please," Wilkins says, calmly. His voice, his demeanor, they have been the whole time. "Tell everyone. Use whatever mechanisms are at your disposal. Mass communications, a press release, email, what's app groups, text chains, phone calls, please, call them, whoever, call them, tell them, now. There's no time to lose."

"Press release," Lucy says, she not calm, but her voice hardly above a whisper. She feels emotionally wrecked, drained, her energy drunk to the dregs by the ongoing vortex of it, she's like bathtub remnants on the way out, the last one-eighth cubic foot of water—now, that's not even a gallon, 0.935 gallons—on spin cycle circling the drain. Oh, she's tried. Oh, her head, my head, she thinks, pinching her nose on the bridge, harder and harder, now really pressing firmly until there she can sense her pulse. "Press release?" she laughs. "Press release, are you, Mark, can I call you Mark?"

Wilkins says nothing.

"Listen, Mark," leaning forward. "It's over. It's all over. My work, my life's work, poof," falling back into her chair as her hands, which had been clasped, come undone then spread out fully extending as far as her wingspan will allow. "I don't know how, I'm saying, what I mean, what I'm trying to say is that I don't know how to convey this to you, to anyone, to, I've just put in every last ounce of everything that I have, I mean all of, all of, everything, all of me into this

town

and so for it to all come apart at the seams the moment when it had first . . . I . . . ," she breaks down and starts crying.

"It's not over, Lucy," Wilkins says. "There's always hope. I'm offering you hope. But you have to act now. You have to tell everyone not to leave. This

town

is a sanctuary and when the storm hits those that are within these walls, so to speak, are going to see the other side of this. And you're going to lead them there, Lucy. But, I beg you, every second counts, act, now."

Lucy looks at him.

"Now, Lucy. Do what you can," he says, now standing up and heading back out the door whence he had come. "Now," he says, a final time.

II.

It's a day later, twenty hours to be precise, since she spoke to Wilkins. Lucy was right, of course, few people heeded her call. And she put out the call, all the calls, every line and without a second of hesitation just like he had demanded she do. Wilkins had left her office and she allowed herself one minute, 90 seconds tops, before flying into this headlong with all her usual gusto, focus, indefatigable energy. She had made all the calls but *head for the hills, the sea, the not here*, that was the general response on the other side of the line. That's what most did in response to her—I mean, she can't be serious—call to stay put, shelter in place, ride out the storm. One can ride out a hurricane and hide underground even underneath the fury of an F-5 tornado. But by now everyone had seen the photos of Syracuse in the aftermath. Everyone had seen the photos of what used to be Chicago. There was no facing this, there was only flight, terrified fleeing best done as quickly as possible.

The

town

has a normal population of about 30,000 people. Two thousand five hundred? maybe not even that much had remained. Dave was still here. He was with his wife until death do us part. And in terms of animals, all the dogs, all the dogs of the

town

who either were strays or had been left behind by their owners in the get out now mayhem were still in

town.

The dogs, they were well represented. Half of the city council, and credit to them, had stayed, with most remaining out of a Captain Edward Smith going down on the Titanic old school, thought of a bygone era, dutiful attachment to the

town

but, most especially, to their Mayor. *I'm with the Mayor no matter what* would be, under normal circumstances, painfully cringe if not downright loathsome in its sticky and syrupy sycophantism.

Here,

now, it was beautiful.

The Dust Plague was but 20 miles east of the

town,

moving at 200 miles per hour, as Lucy and the remaining city council members sat in their usual seats amidst quite a few empty chairs and waited to hear what she was going to say. They were certain, down to the last man, the last woman, that they were here to hear some funeral oration, their own, and were resigned, at least in theory, to their fate, to being sealed in by the dusty winds in this future sarcophagus Mount Vesuvius style in the city center if only to be afterwards dissolved down to elemental foundations by the acid thing, the active ingredient thing.

Yes, they were resigned, and with an austere and Stoic-like bravery. The religious people in the room made their peace with God, the secular people with themselves, and there was a lot of niceness in the room, an outside observer would notice that. A lot of sincere, deep below superficiality, well wishes and thoughts something like "I'll see you in another life," and "we're off to a better place." Even the atheists, this outside observer would notice, even they were trying to go off on a positive note.

Then Lucy spoke and she told them the plan and that the plan was no plan but rather the homeless guy, this homeless guy who was a former congressman, coming to see her, personally, and telling her to tell everyone to stay, that it was going to be alright, but that he offered no explanation, no rational nor scientific nor anything actual reason, why this was the case and that he had then left and that was it, that was the plan or the lack of a plan, and then Lucy made a joke about perspective and how maybe the truest saying in life is that life is what you make of it and why don't we make the most of the few remaining minutes we have left because she, they, all of them in that room, alongside most everyone in the

town,

had no doubt whatsoever that what was about to happen was the logical thing anyone would say would happen to a

town

in the direct, eye of the storm, path of a one hundred mile wide deadly front moving at two hundred miles per hour and so, Lucy suggested, tears coming to her eyes, why don't we, why don't we finish this thing we call life with some love, huh, I love you all, Lucy said, it's been a pleasure, no, you see, it's been the honor of my life, the honor of my life, serving with you. I love you all. And everyone in the room responded in kind and most everyone was crying too, some weeping, some weeping so heavily snot was smearing their face, their shirt sleeves, their eyes.

Lucy pulls out a book from her purse and turns it over a few times in her hands. She lifts it up for all to see. Thoreau's *Walden.* "I think it would be fitting, appropriate, at a time like this, to hear some uplifting words. Even if now, for a final time. Any...," her voice begins to crack. But she had cried enough. Everyone had cried enough. "Any objections?"

Everyone shakes their heads; no, no objections. She opens the book to one of her pre-placed sticky notes, reserved for the real gems, the great not good parts, and reads aloud.

> The mass of men lead lives of quiet desperation. What is called resignation is confirmed desperation. From the desperate city you go into the desperate country, and have to console yourself with the bravery of minks and muskrats. A stereotyped but unconscious despair is concealed even under what are called the games and amusements of mankind. There is no play in them, for this comes after work. But it is a characteristic of wisdom not—

The sound of the room's main door boomerangthwackthwocking off its frame then bouncing back, then once more towards the frame, for it had been opened with considerable force, stops Lucy midsentence and turns the gathered party's collective attention towards the door. There stands one of the seven homeless men, Seraphim, although they do not know his name, he wearing his usual outfit, and he had a beer in his right hand, and he had a beer in his left hand, and on his head that hat, that same hat,

I'VE SUNG IN THE GREATEST CHOIR
IN THE WHOLE UNIVERSE.

They are at rapt attention, looking at him. He has not moved since opening the door and now it is obvious, owing to the beers he is holding, that he had opened it with his foot, kicked it open. They are looking at him and he at them and Lucy looks visibly sad. Did not the universe have the slightest decency to let them die in peace, to allow them at least the smallest autonomy of listening, with no interruptions, to Henry David Thoreau as the storm came and ushered them into eternity? Could not this man, this idiot, just go and stick his head in some toilet, some manhole, bury his head in the sand like an ostrich.

A smile comes to Seraphim's face. He raises his hands, the beer foam higher up than everything, some of it lapping over the mugs and dripping down the slides, as he launches into a burped-out version of the *Star-Spangled Banner.* Right around "Whose broad stripes and bright stars," the groans in the assembly became audible and sustained. Lucy, and she had done such a great job before, she had held back the tears and had been reading Thoreau with the clarity and gentle pace he deserved, buried her head into her hands and began to weep.

Great, just great, she thought, *great, great, great,* with each mental "great" that passed across her internal thoughts she cried all the harder. *Great, I'm going to die, we're all going to die being sent off by a homeless moron burping the national anthem. All my life's work,* she thought, and that was something that had often occupied her thoughts, even in the best of times, her "legacy," the "mark" she would make upon this

town,

how future citizens of this

town

would remember her, and yes, yes she would admit that she had often wondered if one day they'd speak about her in hushed tones, with reverence, she the "best," the "greatest," the "most capable," dare I dream, the most capable Mayor in the history of this

town

and just maybe, why not, when the city council of the future was debating the pros and cons of allocating public funds to build a statue in her honor, well, let me say this, and my grandmother, she was alive way back when, let me tell you, let me say that things were good back then, back when Mayor Lucy was in charge, a splendid era, a golden age, I say, but now, *all my life's work reduced to this most pathetic display of human frailty and I defeated by it. He defeated me*, she kept thinking, *this idiot stole my send off and substituted his.*

And she kept on crying,
he was still burping,
almost done,
but still burping,

and she thought about T. S. Eliot's *The Wasteland* and what the poet would have said if this is the way the world ends, this is the way the world ends, this is the way the world ends, not with a bang but a whimpering homeless drunk burp-singing?

"Look, listen," Seraphim says, speaking for the first time. "Look." He points towards the windows and the assembly follows his finger. The winds outside, they are howling, the wind is verifiably whipping, full on churning, and yet here, inside, it is calm, impossibly calm. Seraphim walks over to the projector and flips it on. Search engine cleared; something typed in, quickly, "search" clicked, a weather site, he scrolls, clicks, a map, and they sit there and look and cannot believe what they were seeing. "Look," Seraphim says, now pointing at the screen. A few years ago, city hall had invested in a state of the art, clean cast, high resolution, audio-visual system. The picture was beautiful, clear, large, it just didn't make sense, it could not be.

They keep looking.

They start murmuring.

A weather map, a radar map, the Dust Plague tracker, and they had seen this before, the past few weeks, ever since Syracuse, for sure, and on these maps the storm was usually portrayed by a blue-purple front with heavy metallic brown, that active ingredient, that acid, the metallic brown all at the center, like an avocado cut in half and at the center of the light green that brown core, impossible to miss, brown, metallic acid, like a leaky battery, a melting battery of pain, like nuclear runoff and a broken sewage pipe, like pain, like putting a new battery to the tongue your tongue and it stings, like getting a wasp sting right on your tongue, soon-quick a big bubble of swollen tongue material, it hurts, it's sensitive to the touch, and so now put that wasp stung tongue to the battery and just ride that pain-buzz sensation down to the last stop on the line, it stings, it hurts, it gets into your nerves, your chord system, it shocks you down to the feet, the soles of your feet, pruny feet left too long in a bathtub when the bath you took was too long, now they're quite worn out, two standard deviations past exfoliation, it tingles your toes, and this whole battery toe buzz brown did look like hurt and pain, it looked painful, even in representation, and it had been like this on maps the whole time but now, on this map, it was all blue-purple.

The storm was here—look outside, howling, still howling, and some hail coming off of it too, spitting off the roof, the windows, the windows, the roof, being pelted, pop, pop, pop like paintballs like stones like pebbles like, pop, pop, pop, over and over, good consistent hail and so much wind—but it looked like a storm, like only, like just, just a storm, and nothing more. But it could not be, it was not to be believed. Once councilman, who had been tracking the storm on his phone, had seen the brown core against the blue-purple but ten minutes ago and he kept refreshing his phone but the brown was gone, and he tried this site then that site, this other radar page, this, even that other thing, but nothing, the brown was gone.

A *breaking news* alert cut into the radar map they were all watching, and a news anchor came onto the screen. She told them what she knew, and this was very much a developing situation, but here are the facts, just the facts: the Dust Plague storm, the one and same one they, and everyone, had been tracking foot by foot, second by second, had inexplicably broken; inexplicably because not only did they, certainly, not have an explanation, but it seemed no one did; and by the way, you saw it too, she said to her viewers, and the equipment, *the* equipment we're talking about now, all this sophisticated weather stuff, it's sensitive down to the split particles; and you saw it, we all did, how the storm full of all that brown stuff stopped being so and while a storm it remained, it was now something, or rather nothing, nothing more than, a normal storm, some wind, some rain, some hail, some gusts but the "apocalypse," or whatever, that, that had been avoided but we, she said, we don't know why, but the thing is, our trusted viewers at Channel ____ here on the 5'oclock news know that as soon as we have something, anything, any new information, you'll be the first to know. For this, she concluded, was very much, if not the textbook definition of, a developing story.

III.

Seraphim turns off the projector. The wind and the rain are still going on fairly intensely outside. Seraphim grabs a chair and sits down. He looks at them, the whole assembly, all that's left of what was once the city council, Lucy too, Lucy especially. They don't speak. He is silent. This goes on for a good ten, fifteen seconds until,

"Wilkins did it," Seraphim says, "Legend."

The assembly is still speechless.

"Wilkins got it done. One man, one guy willing to sacrifice. Legend."

"What are you," Lucy finally manages, "what are you talking about, what do you mean?"

"He told you, didn't he?" Seraphim asks Lucy.

"No," she says, "told me what, no, he came to my office, um, yesterday, he, yes, he told me, he said, he said for me to tell everyone to stay, to not, to not leave. I did. I did that."

"Yes," Seraphim says, "and thank you for doing that. The one thousand, seven hundred, and seventy-seven people left in this

town

are alive thanks to you, and thanks to Wilkins."

"One thousand, seven hundred, and seventy-seven," a councilman says. "Are you serious? One thousand, seven hundred, and seventy-seven! You know the exact number, down to the exact individual. What, next, why don't you tell us how many unique raindrops have fallen in this storm, or–

"Yes," Seraphim says, cutting him off and quieting down the laughter. "One thousand, seven hundred, and seventy-seven. That's right. That's how many people stayed in the

town

and, in doing so, by heeding Lucy's call, and thanks to Wilkins, saved their lives. Those who left, they're dead. People will find all that out soon, you heard the newswoman, they're still piecing together all the loose strands. And, of course, it's a developing situation, like she said, that's true. The storm, that now infamous brown part, went out with a bang. Before it dissipated, as we all saw just now, it split to the sides of us here,

it went into overdrive,

X x x x x x x x x x x 0 0 0 0 0 0 0 0 0 0 x x x x x x
x x x x x x x x x Y Y Y Y Y Y Y Y Y Y Y 2 2 2 2 2 2 2
2 2 2 2 2 2 x x x x x x x x x x x x x x x p p p p p p p
X x x x x x x x x x x 0 0 0 0 0 0 0 0 0 0 x x x x x x

x x x x x x x x Y Y Y Y Y Y Y Y Y Y Y Y 2 2 2 2 2 2 2
2 2 2 2 2 2 x x x x x x x x x x x x x x p p p p p p p
X x x x x x x x x x x 0 0 0 0 0 0 0 0 0 0 x x x x x x
x x x x x x x x Y Y Y Y Y Y Y Y Y Y Y Y 2 2 2 2 2 2 2
2 2 2 2 2 2 x x x x x x x x x x x x x x p p p p p p p
X x x x x x x x x x x 0 0 0 0 0 0 0 0 0 0 x x x x x x
x x x x x x x x Y Y Y Y Y Y Y Y Y Y Y Y 2 2 2 2 2 2 2
2 2 2 2 2 2 x x x x x x x x x x x x x x p p p p p p p
X x x x x x x x x x x 0 0 0 0 0 0 0 0 0 0 x x x x x x
x x x x x x x x Y Y Y Y Y Y Y Y Y Y Y Y 2 2 2 2 2 2 2
2 2 2 2 2 2 x x x x x x x x x x x x x x p p p p p p p
X x x x x x x x x x x 0 0 0 0 0 0 0 0 0 0 x x x x x x
x x x x x x x x Y Y Y Y Y Y Y Y Y Y Y Y 2 2 2 2 2 2 2
2 2 2 2 2 2 x x x x x x x x x x x x x x p p p p p p p
X x x x x x x x x x x 0 0 0 0 0 0 0 0 0 0 x x x x x x
x x x x x x x x Y Y Y Y Y Y Y Y Y Y Y Y 2 2 2 2 2 2 2
2 2 2 2 2 2 x x x x x x x x x x x x x x p p p p p p p
X x x x x x x x x x x 0 0 0 0 0 0 0 0 0 0 x x x x x x
x x x x x x x x Y Y Y Y Y Y Y Y Y Y Y Y 2 2 2 2 2 2 2
2 2 2 2 2 2 x x x x x x x x x x x x x x p p p p p p p
X x x x x x x x x x x 0 0 0 0 0 0 0 0 0 0 x x x x x x
x x x x x x x x Y Y Y Y Y Y Y Y Y Y Y Y 2 2 2 2 2 2 2
2 2 2 2 2 2 x x x x x x x x x x x x x x p p p p p p p
X x x x x x x x x x x 0 0 0 0 0 0 0 0 0 0 x x x x x x
x x x x x x x x Y Y Y Y Y Y Y Y Y Y Y Y 2 2 2 2 2 2 2
2 2 2 2 2 2 x x x x x x x x x x x x x x p p p p p p p
X x x x x x x x x x x 0 0 0 0 0 0 0 0 0 0 x x x x x x
x x x x x x x x Y Y Y Y Y Y Y Y Y Y Y Y 2 2 2 2 2 2 2
2 2 2 2 2 2 x x x x x x x x x x x x x x p p p p p p p
X x x x x x x x x x x 0 0 0 0 0 0 0 0 0 0 x x x x x x
x x x x x x x x Y Y Y Y Y Y Y Y Y Y Y Y 2 2 2 2 2 2 2
2 2 2 2 2 2 x x x x x x x x x x x x x x p p p p p p p
X x x x x x x x x x x 0 0 0 0 0 0 0 0 0 0 x x x x x x
x x x x x x x x Y Y Y Y Y Y Y Y Y Y Y Y 2 2 2 2 2 2 2
2 2 2 2 2 2 x x x x x x x x x x x x x x p p p p p p p
X x x x x x x x x x x 0 0 0 0 0 0 0 0 0 0 x x x x x x
x x x x x x x x Y Y Y Y Y Y Y Y Y Y Y Y 2 2 2 2 2 2 2
2 2 2 2 2 2 x x x x x x x x x x x x x x p p p p p p p
X x x x x x x x x x x 0 0 0 0 0 0 0 0 0 0 x x x x x x
x x x x x x x x Y Y Y Y Y Y Y Y Y Y Y Y 2 2 2 2 2 2 2

2 2 2 2 2 2 x x x x x x x x x x x x x x p p p p p p p
X x x x x x x x x x x 0 0 0 0 0 0 0 0 0 0 x x x x x x
x x x x x x x x Y Y Y Y Y Y Y Y Y Y Y Y 2 2 2 2 2 2 2
2 2 2 2 2 2 x x x x x x x x x x x x x x p p p p p p p
X x x x x x x x x x x 0 0 0 0 0 0 0 0 0 0 x x x x x x
x x x x x x x x Y Y Y Y Y Y Y Y Y Y Y Y 2 2 2 2 2 2 2
2 2 2 2 2 2 x x x x x x x x x x x x x x p p p p p p p
X x x x x x x x x x x 0 0 0 0 0 0 0 0 0 0 x x x x x x
x x x x x x x x Y Y Y Y Y Y Y Y Y Y Y Y 2 2 2 2 2 2 2
2 2 2 2 2 2 x x x x x x x x x x x x x x p p p p p p p
X x x x x x x x x x x 0 0 0 0 0 0 0 0 0 0 x x x x x x
x x x x x x x x Y Y Y Y Y Y Y Y Y Y Y Y 2 2 2 2 2 2 2
2 2 2 2 2 2 x x x x x x x x x x x x x x p p p p p p p
X x x x x x x x x x x 0 0 0 0 0 0 0 0 0 0 x x x x x x
x x x x x x x x Y Y Y Y Y Y Y Y Y Y Y Y 2 2 2 2 2 2 2
2 2 2 2 2 2 x x x x x x x x x x x x x x p p p p p p p
X x x x x x x x x x x 0 0 0 0 0 0 0 0 0 0 x x x x x x
x x x x x x x x Y Y Y Y Y Y Y Y Y Y Y Y 2 2 2 2 2 2 2
2 2 2 2 2 2 x x x x x x x x x x x x x x p p p p p p p
X x x x x x x x x x x 0 0 0 0 0 0 0 0 0 0 x x x x x x
x x x x x x x x Y Y Y Y Y Y Y Y Y Y Y Y 2 2 2 2 2 2 2
2 2 2 2 2 2 x x x x x x x x x x x x x x p p p p p p p
X x x x x x x x x x x 0 0 0 0 0 0 0 0 0 0 x x x x x x
x x x x x x x x Y Y Y Y Y Y Y Y Y Y Y Y 2 2 2 2 2 2 2
2 2 2 2 2 2 x x x x x x x x x x x x x x p p p p p p p
X x x x x x x x x x x 0 0 0 0 0 0 0 0 0 0 x x x x x x
x x x x x x x x Y Y Y Y Y Y Y Y Y Y Y Y 2 2 2 2 2 2 2
2 2 2 2 2 2 x x x x x x x x x x x x x x p p p p p p p
X x x x x x x x x x x 0 0 0 0 0 0 0 0 0 0 x x x x x x
x x x x x x x x Y Y Y Y Y Y Y Y Y Y Y Y 2 2 2 2 2 2 2
2 2 2 2 2 2 x x x x x x x x x x x x x x p p p p p p p
X x x x x x x x x x x 0 0 0 0 0 0 0 0 0 0 x x x x x x
x x x x x x x x Y Y Y Y Y Y Y Y Y Y Y Y 2 2 2 2 2 2 2
2 2 2 2 2 2 x x x x x x x x x x x x x x p p p p p p p
X x x x x x x x x x x 0 0 0 0 0 0 0 0 0 0 x x x x x x
x x x x x x x x Y Y Y Y Y Y Y Y Y Y Y Y 2 2 2 2 2 2 2
2 2 2 2 2 2 x x x x x x x x x x x x x x p p p p p p p
X x x x x x x x x x x 0 0 0 0 0 0 0 0 0 0 x x x x x x
x x x x x x x x Y Y Y Y Y Y Y Y Y Y Y Y 2 2 2 2 2 2 2
2 2 2 2 2 2 x x x x x x x x x x x x x x p p p p p p p

X x x x x x x x x x x 0 0 0 0 0 0 0 0 0 0 x x x x x x
x x x x x x x x Y Y Y Y Y Y Y Y Y Y Y Y 2 2 2 2 2 2 2
2 2 2 2 2 2 x x x x x x x x x x x x x x p p p p p p p
X x x x x x x x x x x 0 0 0 0 0 0 0 0 0 0 x x x x x x
x x x x x x x x Y Y Y Y Y Y Y Y Y Y Y Y 2 2 2 2 2 2 2
2 2 2 2 2 2 x x x x x x x x x x x x x x p p p p p p p
X x x x x x x x x x x 0 0 0 0 0 0 0 0 0 0 x x x x x x
x x x x x x x x Y Y Y Y Y Y Y Y Y Y Y Y 2 2 2 2 2 2 2
2 2 2 2 2 2 x x x x x x x x x x x x x x p p p p p p p
X x x x x x x x x x x 0 0 0 0 0 0 0 0 0 0 x x x x x x
x x x x x x x x Y Y Y Y Y Y Y Y Y Y Y Y 2 2 2 2 2 2 2
2 2 2 2 2 2 x x x x x x x x x x x x x x p p p p p p p
X x x x x x x x x x x 0 0 0 0 0 0 0 0 0 0 x x x x x x
x x x x x x x x Y Y Y Y Y Y Y Y Y Y Y Y 2 2 2 2 2 2 2
2 2 2 2 2 2 x x x x x x x x x x x x x x p p p p p p p
X x x x x x x x x x x 0 0 0 0 0 0 0 0 0 0 x x x x x x
x x x x x x x x Y Y Y Y Y Y Y Y Y Y Y Y 2 2 2 2 2 2 2
2 2 2 2 2 2 x x x x x x x x x x x x x x p p p p p p p
X x x x x x x x x x x 0 0 0 0 0 0 0 0 0 0 x x x x x x
x x x x x x x x Y Y Y Y Y Y Y Y Y Y Y Y 2 2 2 2 2 2 2
2 2 2 2 2 2 x x x x x x x x x x x x x x p p p p p p p
X x x x x x x x x x x 0 0 0 0 0 0 0 0 0 0 x x x x x x
x x x x x x x x Y Y Y Y Y Y Y Y Y Y Y Y 2 2 2 2 2 2 2
2 2 2 2 2 2 x x x x x x x x x x x x x x p p p p p p p
X x x x x x x x x x x 0 0 0 0 0 0 0 0 0 0 x x x x x x
x x x x x x x x Y Y Y Y Y Y Y Y Y Y Y Y 2 2 2 2 2 2 2
2 2 2 2 2 2 x x x x x x x x x x x x x x p p p p p p p
X x x x x x x x x x x 0 0 0 0 0 0 0 0 0 0 x x x x x x
x x x x x x x x Y Y Y Y Y Y Y Y Y Y Y Y 2 2 2 2 2 2 2
2 2 2 2 2 2 x x x x x x x x x x x x x x p p p p p p p
X x x x x x x x x x x 0 0 0 0 0 0 0 0 0 0 x x x x x x
x x x x x x x x Y Y Y Y Y Y Y Y Y Y Y Y 2 2 2 2 2 2 2
2 2 2 2 2 2 x x x x x x x x x x x x x x p p p p p p p
X x x x x x x x x x x 0 0 0 0 0 0 0 0 0 0 x x x x x x
x x x x x x x x Y Y Y Y Y Y Y Y Y Y Y Y 2 2 2 2 2 2 2
2 2 2 2 2 2 x x x x x x x x x x x x x x p p p p p p p

hypermax winds,

X x x x x x x x x x x 0 0 0 0 0 0 0 0 0 0 x x x x x x
x x x x x x x x Y Y Y Y Y Y Y Y Y Y Y Y 2 2 2 2 2 2 2
2 2 2 2 2 2 x x x x x x x x x x x x x x p p p p p p p

X x x x x x x x x x x 0 0 0 0 0 0 0 0 0 0 x x x x x x
x x x x x x x x Y Y Y Y Y Y Y Y Y Y Y Y 2 2 2 2 2 2 2
2 2 2 2 2 2 x x x x x x x x x x x x x x p p p p p p p
X x x x x x x x x x x 0 0 0 0 0 0 0 0 0 0 x x x x x x
x x x x x x x x Y Y Y Y Y Y Y Y Y Y Y Y 2 2 2 2 2 2 2
2 2 2 2 2 2 x x x x x x x x x x x x x x p p p p p p p
X x x x x x x x x x x 0 0 0 0 0 0 0 0 0 0 x x x x x x
x x x x x x x x Y Y Y Y Y Y Y Y Y Y Y Y 2 2 2 2 2 2 2
2 2 2 2 2 2 x x x x x x x x x x x x x x p p p p p p p
X x x x x x x x x x x 0 0 0 0 0 0 0 0 0 0 x x x x x x
x x x x x x x x Y Y Y Y Y Y Y Y Y Y Y Y 2 2 2 2 2 2 2
2 2 2 2 2 2 x x x x x x x x x x x x x x p p p p p p p
X x x x x x x x x x x 0 0 0 0 0 0 0 0 0 0 x x x x x x
x x x x x x x x Y Y Y Y Y Y Y Y Y Y Y Y 2 2 2 2 2 2 2
2 2 2 2 2 2 x x x x x x x x x x x x x x p p p p p p p
X x x x x x x x x x x 0 0 0 0 0 0 0 0 0 0 x x x x x x
x x x x x x x x Y Y Y Y Y Y Y Y Y Y Y Y 2 2 2 2 2 2 2
2 2 2 2 2 2 x x x x x x x x x x x x x x p p p p p p p
X x x x x x x x x x x 0 0 0 0 0 0 0 0 0 0 x x x x x x
x x x x x x x x Y Y Y Y Y Y Y Y Y Y Y Y 2 2 2 2 2 2 2
2 2 2 2 2 2 x x x x x x x x x x x x x x p p p p p p p
X x x x x x x x x x x 0 0 0 0 0 0 0 0 0 0 x x x x x x
x x x x x x x x Y Y Y Y Y Y Y Y Y Y Y Y 2 2 2 2 2 2 2
2 2 2 2 2 2 x x x x x x x x x x x x x x p p p p p p p
X x x x x x x x x x x 0 0 0 0 0 0 0 0 0 0 x x x x x x
x x x x x x x x Y Y Y Y Y Y Y Y Y Y Y Y 2 2 2 2 2 2 2
2 2 2 2 2 2 x x x x x x x x x x x x x x p p p p p p p
X x x x x x x x x x x 0 0 0 0 0 0 0 0 0 0 x x x x x x
x x x x x x x x Y Y Y Y Y Y Y Y Y Y Y Y 2 2 2 2 2 2 2
2 2 2 2 2 2 x x x x x x x x x x x x x x p p p p p p p
X x x x x x x x x x x 0 0 0 0 0 0 0 0 0 0 x x x x x x
x x x x x x x x Y Y Y Y Y Y Y Y Y Y Y Y 2 2 2 2 2 2 2
2 2 2 2 2 2 x x x x x x x x x x x x x x p p p p p p p
X x x x x x x x x x x 0 0 0 0 0 0 0 0 0 0 x x x x x x
x x x x x x x x Y Y Y Y Y Y Y Y Y Y Y Y 2 2 2 2 2 2 2
2 2 2 2 2 2 x x x x x x x x x x x x x x p p p p p p p
X x x x x x x x x x x 0 0 0 0 0 0 0 0 0 0 x x x x x x
x x x x x x x x Y Y Y Y Y Y Y Y Y Y Y Y 2 2 2 2 2 2 2
2 2 2 2 2 2 x x x x x x x x x x x x x x p p p p p p p
X x x x x x x x x x x 0 0 0 0 0 0 0 0 0 0 x x x x x x
x x x x x x x x Y Y Y Y Y Y Y Y Y Y Y Y 2 2 2 2 2 2 2
2 2 2 2 2 2 x x x x x x x x x x x x x x p p p p p p p
X x x x x x x x x x x 0 0 0 0 0 0 0 0 0 0 x x x x x x
x x x x x x x x Y Y Y Y Y Y Y Y Y Y Y Y 2 2 2 2 2 2 2

2 2 2 2 2 2 x x x x x x x x x x x x x x p p p p p p p
X x x x x x x x x x x 0 0 0 0 0 0 0 0 0 0 x x x x x x
x x x x x x x x Y Y Y Y Y Y Y Y Y Y Y Y 2 2 2 2 2 2 2
2 2 2 2 2 2 x x x x x x x x x x x x x x p p p p p p p
X x x x x x x x x x x 0 0 0 0 0 0 0 0 0 0 x x x x x x
x x x x x x x x Y Y Y Y Y Y Y Y Y Y Y Y 2 2 2 2 2 2 2
2 2 2 2 2 2 x x x x x x x x x x x x x x p p p p p p p
X x x x x x x x x x x 0 0 0 0 0 0 0 0 0 0 x x x x x x
x x x x x x x x Y Y Y Y Y Y Y Y Y Y Y Y 2 2 2 2 2 2 2
2 2 2 2 2 2 x x x x x x x x x x x x x x p p p p p p p
X x x x x x x x x x x 0 0 0 0 0 0 0 0 0 0 x x x x x x
x x x x x x x x Y Y Y Y Y Y Y Y Y Y Y Y 2 2 2 2 2 2 2
2 2 2 2 2 2 x x x x x x x x x x x x x x p p p p p p p
X x x x x x x x x x x 0 0 0 0 0 0 0 0 0 0 x x x x x x
x x x x x x x x Y Y Y Y Y Y Y Y Y Y Y Y 2 2 2 2 2 2 2
2 2 2 2 2 2 x x x x x x x x x x x x x x p p p p p p p
X x x x x x x x x x x 0 0 0 0 0 0 0 0 0 0 x x x x x x
x x x x x x x x Y Y Y Y Y Y Y Y Y Y Y Y 2 2 2 2 2 2 2
2 2 2 2 2 2 x x x x x x x x x x x x x x p p p p p p p
X x x x x x x x x x x 0 0 0 0 0 0 0 0 0 0 x x x x x x
x x x x x x x x Y Y Y Y Y Y Y Y Y Y Y Y 2 2 2 2 2 2 2
2 2 2 2 2 2 x x x x x x x x x x x x x x p p p p p p p
X x x x x x x x x x x 0 0 0 0 0 0 0 0 0 0 x x x x x x
x x x x x x x x Y Y Y Y Y Y Y Y Y Y Y Y 2 2 2 2 2 2 2
2 2 2 2 2 2 x x x x x x x x x x x x x x p p p p p p p
X x x x x x x x x x x 0 0 0 0 0 0 0 0 0 0 x x x x x x
x x x x x x x x Y Y Y Y Y Y Y Y Y Y Y Y 2 2 2 2 2 2 2
2 2 2 2 2 2 x x x x x x x x x x x x x x p p p p p p p
X x x x x x x x x x x 0 0 0 0 0 0 0 0 0 0 x x x x x x
x x x x x x x x Y Y Y Y Y Y Y Y Y Y Y Y 2 2 2 2 2 2 2
2 2 2 2 2 2 x x x x x x x x x x x x x x p p p p p p p
X x x x x x x x x x x 0 0 0 0 0 0 0 0 0 0 x x x x x x
x x x x x x x x Y Y Y Y Y Y Y Y Y Y Y Y 2 2 2 2 2 2 2
2 2 2 2 2 2 x x x x x x x x x x x x x x p p p p p p p
X x x x x x x x x x x 0 0 0 0 0 0 0 0 0 0 x x x x x x
x x x x x x x x Y Y Y Y Y Y Y Y Y Y Y Y 2 2 2 2 2 2 2
2 2 2 2 2 2 x x x x x x x x x x x x x x p p p p p p p
X x x x x x x x x x x 0 0 0 0 0 0 0 0 0 0 x x x x x x
x x x x x x x x Y Y Y Y Y Y Y Y Y Y Y Y 2 2 2 2 2 2 2
2 2 2 2 2 2 x x x x x x x x x x x x x x p p p p p p p
X x x x x x x x x x x 0 0 0 0 0 0 0 0 0 0 x x x x x x
x x x x x x x x Y Y Y Y Y Y Y Y Y Y Y Y 2 2 2 2 2 2 2
2 2 2 2 2 2 x x x x x x x x x x x x x x p p p p p p p

X x x x x x x x x x x 0 0 0 0 0 0 0 0 0 0 x x x x x x
x x x x x x x x Y Y Y Y Y Y Y Y Y Y Y Y 2 2 2 2 2 2 2
2 2 2 2 2 2 x x x x x x x x x x x x x x p p p p p p p
X x x x x x x x x x x 0 0 0 0 0 0 0 0 0 0 x x x x x x
x x x x x x x x Y Y Y Y Y Y Y Y Y Y Y Y 2 2 2 2 2 2 2
2 2 2 2 2 2 x x x x x x x x x x x x x x p p p p p p p
X x x x x x x x x x x 0 0 0 0 0 0 0 0 0 0 x x x x x x
x x x x x x x x Y Y Y Y Y Y Y Y Y Y Y Y 2 2 2 2 2 2 2
2 2 2 2 2 2 x x x x x x x x x x x x x x p p p p p p p
X x x x x x x x x x x 0 0 0 0 0 0 0 0 0 0 x x x x x x
x x x x x x x x Y Y Y Y Y Y Y Y Y Y Y Y 2 2 2 2 2 2 2
2 2 2 2 2 2 x x x x x x x x x x x x x x p p p p p p p
X x x x x x x x x x x 0 0 0 0 0 0 0 0 0 0 x x x x x x
x x x x x x x x Y Y Y Y Y Y Y Y Y Y Y Y 2 2 2 2 2 2 2
2 2 2 2 2 2 x x x x x x x x x x x x x x p p p p p p p
X x x x x x x x x x x 0 0 0 0 0 0 0 0 0 0 x x x x x x
x x x x x x x x Y Y Y Y Y Y Y Y Y Y Y Y 2 2 2 2 2 2 2
2 2 2 2 2 2 x x x x x x x x x x x x x x p p p p p p p
X x x x x x x x x x x 0 0 0 0 0 0 0 0 0 0 x x x x x x
x x x x x x x x Y Y Y Y Y Y Y Y Y Y Y Y 2 2 2 2 2 2 2
2 2 2 2 2 2 x x x x x x x x x x x x x x p p p p p p p
X x x x x x x x x x x 0 0 0 0 0 0 0 0 0 0 x x x x x x
x x x x x x x x Y Y Y Y Y Y Y Y Y Y Y Y 2 2 2 2 2 2 2
2 2 2 2 2 2 x x x x x x x x x x x x x x p p p p p p p
X x x x x x x x x x x 0 0 0 0 0 0 0 0 0 0 x x x x x x
x x x x x x x x Y Y Y Y Y Y Y Y Y Y Y Y 2 2 2 2 2 2 2
2 2 2 2 2 2 x x x x x x x x x x x x x x p p p p p p p
X x x x x x x x x x x 0 0 0 0 0 0 0 0 0 0 x x x x x x
x x x x x x x x Y Y Y Y Y Y Y Y Y Y Y Y 2 2 2 2 2 2 2
2 2 2 2 2 2 x x x x x x x x x x x x x x p p p p p p p

poisonous dust funnels

X x x x x x x x x x x 0 0 0 0 0 0 0 0 0 0 x x x x x x
x x x x x x x x Y Y Y Y Y Y Y Y Y Y Y Y 2 2 2 2 2 2 2
2 2 2 2 2 2 x x x x x x x x x x x x x x p p p p p p p
X x x x x x x x x x x 0 0 0 0 0 0 0 0 0 0 x x x x x x
x x x x x x x x Y Y Y Y Y Y Y Y Y Y Y Y 2 2 2 2 2 2 2
2 2 2 2 2 2 x x x x x x x x x x x x x x p p p p p p p
X x x x x x x x x x x 0 0 0 0 0 0 0 0 0 0 x x x x x x
x x x x x x x x Y Y Y Y Y Y Y Y Y Y Y Y 2 2 2 2 2 2 2
2 2 2 2 2 2 x x x x x x x x x x x x x x p p p p p p p
X x x x x x x x x x x 0 0 0 0 0 0 0 0 0 0 x x x x x x
x x x x x x x x Y Y Y Y Y Y Y Y Y Y Y Y 2 2 2 2 2 2 2

2 2 2 2 2 2 x x x x x x x x x x x x x x p p p p p p p
X x x x x x x x x x x 0 0 0 0 0 0 0 0 0 0 x x x x x x
x x x x x x x x Y Y Y Y Y Y Y Y Y Y Y Y 2 2 2 2 2 2 2
2 2 2 2 2 2 x x x x x x x x x x x x x x p p p p p p p
X x x x x x x x x x x 0 0 0 0 0 0 0 0 0 0 x x x x x x
x x x x x x x x Y Y Y Y Y Y Y Y Y Y Y Y 2 2 2 2 2 2 2
2 2 2 2 2 2 x x x x x x x x x x x x x x p p p p p p p
X x x x x x x x x x x 0 0 0 0 0 0 0 0 0 0 x x x x x x
x x x x x x x x Y Y Y Y Y Y Y Y Y Y Y Y 2 2 2 2 2 2 2
2 2 2 2 2 2 x x x x x x x x x x x x x x p p p p p p p
X x x x x x x x x x x 0 0 0 0 0 0 0 0 0 0 x x x x x x
x x x x x x x x Y Y Y Y Y Y Y Y Y Y Y Y 2 2 2 2 2 2 2
2 2 2 2 2 2 x x x x x x x x x x x x x x p p p p p p p
X x x x x x x x x x x 0 0 0 0 0 0 0 0 0 0 x x x x x x
x x x x x x x x Y Y Y Y Y Y Y Y Y Y Y Y 2 2 2 2 2 2 2
2 2 2 2 2 2 x x x x x x x x x x x x x x p p p p p p p
X x x x x x x x x x x 0 0 0 0 0 0 0 0 0 0 x x x x x x
x x x x x x x x Y Y Y Y Y Y Y Y Y Y Y Y 2 2 2 2 2 2 2
2 2 2 2 2 2 x x x x x x x x x x x x x x p p p p p p p
X x x x x x x x x x x 0 0 0 0 0 0 0 0 0 0 x x x x x x
x x x x x x x x Y Y Y Y Y Y Y Y Y Y Y Y 2 2 2 2 2 2 2
2 2 2 2 2 2 x x x x x x x x x x x x x x p p p p p p p
X x x x x x x x x x x 0 0 0 0 0 0 0 0 0 0 x x x x x x
x x x x x x x x Y Y Y Y Y Y Y Y Y Y Y Y 2 2 2 2 2 2 2
2 2 2 2 2 2 x x x x x x x x x x x x x x p p p p p p p
X x x x x x x x x x x 0 0 0 0 0 0 0 0 0 0 x x x x x x
x x x x x x x x Y Y Y Y Y Y Y Y Y Y Y Y 2 2 2 2 2 2 2
2 2 2 2 2 2 x x x x x x x x x x x x x x p p p p p p p
X x x x x x x x x x x 0 0 0 0 0 0 0 0 0 0 x x x x x x
x x x x x x x x Y Y Y Y Y Y Y Y Y Y Y Y 2 2 2 2 2 2 2
2 2 2 2 2 2 x x x x x x x x x x x x x x p p p p p p p
X x x x x x x x x x x 0 0 0 0 0 0 0 0 0 0 x x x x x x
x x x x x x x x Y Y Y Y Y Y Y Y Y Y Y Y 2 2 2 2 2 2 2
2 2 2 2 2 2 x x x x x x x x x x x x x x p p p p p p p
X x x x x x x x x x x 0 0 0 0 0 0 0 0 0 0 x x x x x x
x x x x x x x x Y Y Y Y Y Y Y Y Y Y Y Y 2 2 2 2 2 2 2
2 2 2 2 2 2 x x x x x x x x x x x x x x p p p p p p p
X x x x x x x x x x x 0 0 0 0 0 0 0 0 0 0 x x x x x x
x x x x x x x x Y Y Y Y Y Y Y Y Y Y Y Y 2 2 2 2 2 2 2
2 2 2 2 2 2 x x x x x x x x x x x x x x p p p p p p p

X x x x x x x x x x x 0 0 0 0 0 0 0 0 0 0 x x x x x x
x x x x x x x x Y Y Y Y Y Y Y Y Y Y Y Y 2 2 2 2 2 2 2
2 2 2 2 2 2 x x x x x x x x x x x x x x p p p p p p p
X x x x x x x x x x x 0 0 0 0 0 0 0 0 0 0 x x x x x x
x x x x x x x x Y Y Y Y Y Y Y Y Y Y Y Y 2 2 2 2 2 2 2
2 2 2 2 2 2 x x x x x x x x x x x x x x p p p p p p p
X x x x x x x x x x x 0 0 0 0 0 0 0 0 0 0 x x x x x x
x x x x x x x x Y Y Y Y Y Y Y Y Y Y Y Y 2 2 2 2 2 2 2
2 2 2 2 2 2 x x x x x x x x x x x x x x p p p p p p p
X x x x x x x x x x x 0 0 0 0 0 0 0 0 0 0 x x x x x x
x x x x x x x x Y Y Y Y Y Y Y Y Y Y Y Y 2 2 2 2 2 2 2
2 2 2 2 2 2 x x x x x x x x x x x x x x p p p p p p p
X x x x x x x x x x x 0 0 0 0 0 0 0 0 0 0 x x x x x x
x x x x x x x x Y Y Y Y Y Y Y Y Y Y Y Y 2 2 2 2 2 2 2
2 2 2 2 2 2 x x x x x x x x x x x x x x p p p p p p p
X x x x x x x x x x x 0 0 0 0 0 0 0 0 0 0 x x x x x x
x x x x x x x x Y Y Y Y Y Y Y Y Y Y Y Y 2 2 2 2 2 2 2
2 2 2 2 2 2 x x x x x x x x x x x x x x p p p p p p p
X x x x x x x x x x x 0 0 0 0 0 0 0 0 0 0 x x x x x x
x x x x x x x x Y Y Y Y Y Y Y Y Y Y Y Y 2 2 2 2 2 2 2
2 2 2 2 2 2 x x x x x x x x x x x x x x p p p p p p p
X x x x x x x x x x x 0 0 0 0 0 0 0 0 0 0 x x x x x x
x x x x x x x x Y Y Y Y Y Y Y Y Y Y Y Y 2 2 2 2 2 2 2
2 2 2 2 2 2 x x x x x x x x x x x x x x p p p p p p p
X x x x x x x x x x x 0 0 0 0 0 0 0 0 0 0 x x x x x x
x x x x x x x x Y Y Y Y Y Y Y Y Y Y Y Y 2 2 2 2 2 2 2
2 2 2 2 2 2 x x x x x x x x x x x x x x p p p p p p p
X x x x x x x x x x x 0 0 0 0 0 0 0 0 0 0 x x x x x x
x x x x x x x x Y Y Y Y Y Y Y Y Y Y Y Y 2 2 2 2 2 2 2
2 2 2 2 2 2 x x x x x x x x x x x x x x p p p p p p p
X x x x x x x x x x x 0 0 0 0 0 0 0 0 0 0 x x x x x x
x x x x x x x x Y Y Y Y Y Y Y Y Y Y Y Y 2 2 2 2 2 2 2
2 2 2 2 2 2 x x x x x x x x x x x x x x p p p p p p p
X x x x x x x x x x x 0 0 0 0 0 0 0 0 0 0 x x x x x x
x x x x x x x x Y Y Y Y Y Y Y Y Y Y Y Y 2 2 2 2 2 2 2
2 2 2 2 2 2 x x x x x x x x x x x x x x p p p p p p p
X x x x x x x x x x x 0 0 0 0 0 0 0 0 0 0 x x x x x x
x x x x x x x x Y Y Y Y Y Y Y Y Y Y Y Y 2 2 2 2 2 2 2
2 2 2 2 2 2 x x x x x x x x x x x x x x p p p p p p p
X x x x x x x x x x x 0 0 0 0 0 0 0 0 0 0 x x x x x x

x x x x x x x x Y Y Y Y Y Y Y Y Y Y Y Y 2 2 2 2 2 2 2

2 2 2 2 2 2 x x x x x x x x x x x x x x p p p p p p p

X x x x x x x x x x x 0 0 0 0 0 0 0 0 0 0 x x x x x x

x x x x x x x x Y Y Y Y Y Y Y Y Y Y Y Y 2 2 2 2 2 2 2

2 2 2 2 2 2 x x x x x x x x x x x x x x p p p p p p p

X x x x x x x x x x x 0 0 0 0 0 0 0 0 0 0 x x x x x x

x x x x x x x x Y Y Y Y Y Y Y Y Y Y Y Y 2 2 2 2 2 2 2

2 2 2 2 2 2 x x x x x x x x x x x x x x p p p p p p p

X x x x x x x x x x x 0 0 0 0 0 0 0 0 0 0 x x x x x x

x x x x x x x x Y Y Y Y Y Y Y Y Y Y Y Y 2 2 2 2 2 2 2

2 2 2 2 2 2 x x x x x x x x x x x x x x p p p p p p p

X x x x x x x x x x x 0 0 0 0 0 0 0 0 0 0 x x x x x x

x x x x x x x x Y Y Y Y Y Y Y Y Y Y Y Y 2 2 2 2 2 2 2

2 2 2 2 2 2 x x x x x x x x x x x x x x p p p p p p p

X x x x x x x x x x x 0 0 0 0 0 0 0 0 0 0 x x x x x x

x x x x x x x x Y Y Y Y Y Y Y Y Y Y Y Y 2 2 2 2 2 2 2

2 2 2 2 2 2 x x x x x x x x x x x x x x p p p p p p p

X x x x x x x x x x x 0 0 0 0 0 0 0 0 0 0 x x x x x x

x x x x x x x x Y Y Y Y Y Y Y Y Y Y Y Y 2 2 2 2 2 2 2

2 2 2 2 2 2 x x x x x x x x x x x x x x p p p p p p p

X x x x x x x x x x x 0 0 0 0 0 0 0 0 0 0 x x x x x x

x x x x x x x x Y Y Y Y Y Y Y Y Y Y Y Y 2 2 2 2 2 2 2

2 2 2 2 2 2 x x x x x x x x x x x x x x p p p p p p p

X x x x x x x x x x x 0 0 0 0 0 0 0 0 0 0 x x x x x x

x x x x x x x x Y Y Y Y Y Y Y Y Y Y Y Y 2 2 2 2 2 2 2

2 2 2 2 2 2 x x x x x x x x x x x x x x p p p p p p p

X x x x x x x x x x x 0 0 0 0 0 0 0 0 0 0 x x x x x x

x x x x x x x x Y Y Y Y Y Y Y Y Y Y Y Y 2 2 2 2 2 2 2

2 2 2 2 2 2 x x x x x x x x x x x x x x p p p p p p p

X x x x x x x x x x x 0 0 0 0 0 0 0 0 0 0 x x x x x x

x x x x x x x x Y Y Y Y Y Y Y Y Y Y Y Y 2 2 2 2 2 2 2

2 2 2 2 2 2 x x x x x x x x x x x x x x p p p p p p p

X x x x x x x x x x x 0 0 0 0 0 0 0 0 0 0 x x x x x x

x x x x x x x x Y Y Y Y Y Y Y Y Y Y Y Y 2 2 2 2 2 2 2

2 2 2 2 2 2 x x x x x x x x x x x x x x p p p p p p p

and it caught them all, all those people trying to flee to the coast, the south, the hills, hide in valleys, it got them. May they rest in peace;

God rest their souls."

"Okay, okay, okay," another council member says. "I, for one, have had enough. Enough of this nonsense! Enough! You," he now standing, pointing at Seraphim in an accusatory fashion, "you, I regret to say, are little more, nothing more than some drunk homeless bum! You and your lot, since you showed up, since you arrived here," he drags out the word arrived, for emphasis, it comes out like *ar-eye-iiii-v'd,* "have contributed nothing, done nothing, added nothing, polluted everything and simply by your presence. You, sir, and I do hate to use the word 'sir,' but you, you and your lot are worse than any 'Dust Plague' what have you and now, haven't we suffered enough? Our little

town

life, our keep to ourselves, hardworking, bother no one, beautiful small life first ruined by you showing up and now we've been through a natural disaster like no one has ever seen, terror and horror and you, you!, you show up here burping your way through the door, talking nonsense, jibber jabbering you and us, all of us, into oblivion, these, these, these pseudo-prophecies of yours, two cent and two bit charlatanism, pretending, and you have the gall, the gall, to pretend to know what has happened to those who left, this, you, this, I have had enough!"

Seraphim says nothing. Another council member raises her hand. A time like this, emotions like this, who says decorum and class have to go by the wayside. She appears to be waiting to be called on.

And so Seraphim does.

"Who is Wilkins?" she asks. "You keep mentioning 'Wilkins'."

"Mark Wilkins," Seraphim replies. "The former congressman. He was here all along, *in cognito* but hiding in plain sight, sitting out there, he was the first of the 'homeless' to arrive."

There is loud and buzzing murmuring about the assembly now. Seraphim continues,

"He got it done. He saved this
town."

"Can you," the same woman asks, she of the formerly raised hand waiting to be called on, "can you please explain, uhm, how, exactly?"

"Yes," Seraphim says. "God asked him to."

The man who had previously had "enough" angrily gets up from his seat and storms out of the room. They are buzzing in murmur once more.

"Please," Lucy says, then slapping the table with her bare palm, twice, "please, let him explain... just let him explain."

"Thank you," Seraphim says. "God asked him to do this. God sent an angel, me, with the following instructions. To ask something of Mark Wilkins, former congressman, and as such, as you know, a man of great worldly success and acclaim, even amongst his detractors, a man, who when I went to see him with this proposal was living a retired life, retired at 48, in great luxury; a hundred plus acre farm in Central Washington, had just become a majority partner in a successful winery near Yakima, was mulling over a seven figure plus offer to become president of Washington State University, the details were still being hammered out but the board in Pullman wanted him, and for him, it was some kind of back and forth to stay here on the farm, check up on the wines once a week, and cash in on his speaking fees whenever he felt like it—$100,000 per appearance, that's the kind of money people were willing to shell out to hear him give a motivational speech, a here's how you do it thing, one afternoon, 100 grand, and he actually got a quarter of a million last year to do that for some bank in New York—or come to Pullman, be university president, the good life here, the good life there, a win-win, can't go wrong.

God sent me to ask him to give it all up.

Give it all up, humiliate yourself, become the lowest of the low, at least to outside appearances, then die. The reward? Straight to heaven, not just forgiveness of his sins, and let me tell you, they were grave and numerous, full forgiveness, a plenary indulgence and, better yet, for as you might have heard once, no man has greater love than this: to lay down his life for his friends, he would save all the people who stayed in this

town

from the coming disaster."

The murmuring is full on talking now, arguing, some people are getting really upset, rather, they are already very upset, and once more, Lucy, who is listening with great attention, has to bring order to the room. Everything might be over now, the whole

town

and city council stuff, or, wait, on second thought, no, maybe it's not, or, maybe for a third time, it is as in it is *now* and later on TBD, but still, yes, and now this for sure, in all three potentialities and however many hypothetical more, once thing is clear: Lucy holds real authority. She says be quiet and they listen. Seraphim resumes speaking,

"I understand so much of this makes no sense to you. Here's the whole recap, and I'll be as to the point as I can.

God sent me, an angel, to a man, Mark Wilkins, a former congressman fallen away Catholic, to offer him a proposal of salvation, a proposal to save his own soul and the lives of many more.

God respects our free will.

Wilkins could have said no.

And please understand, if he said no it's not that now he's going to be damned or now he is responsible for the deaths of the people he could have saved. No, the Dust Plague, as you call it, was coming. This was a most special offer, like I said before, that if you do this, and few people, almost no one, ever, is asked to do this, not only do you become responsible for others' lives, here in a good way, you *are* the hero who saved them but, most importantly, you receive the only reward there is, the eye has not seen, ear has not heard reward.

Wilkins said yes.

He didn't even need much time to think about it.

Yes, he said.

And he said yes, he explained to me, because I, this angel,

was the confirmation of faith he had long been looking for and for which he had long given up hope finding.

Wilkins had lost the faith.

God does not exist,

he became convinced, and so

all the women, the money, the scandals, some of them public knowledge but many more about which no one knows, all that was simply the rational actions of a man using his reason, as he believed, logically. God does not exist, therefore sin is not real, therefore I'm going to get what I can while I can. This is logical, rather it would be, if God did not exist.

But He does exist.

And I was the proof he needed and I saw, that day I met him and proposed this to him, I saw not just repentance in his eyes but joy, a joy not just of faith or belief or hope but facts, St. Thomas My Lord and My God falling to his knees because he had put his hand in his side, his fingers on the nail marks, do you understand what I'm saying? I look around this room and I see people riddled with doubt, overwhelmed by it. I can see your souls, I can see the despair, the radical refusal to believe, in so many of you. And I'm telling you that that was what did it for him, Wilkins. He too did not believe, and while that saddened him, it made sense, too, for it seemed belief was foolish and so he had been living his life in this kind of quiet resignation to nothing. I gotta say, Lucy, that reading you did before, spot on, spot on. And then, it all changed, then, you mean, this is all real, you mean it's actually as in *really* real? So I do think what came next was not that hard for him, for like I said, now he was no longer living in the expectant hope of faith, no matter how firm, no, now he was confirmed in the factual reality of what faith proposed. Now,

he was one of those extremely rare human
beings who was allowed, by God's grace,
to know it was true not just believe.

What came next was him selling everything he had and giving it all away. It was a nice haul, the total donations, and it really was here, there, everywhere, over fifteen million dollars in sum. Having turned to God, having become perfectly materially poor so as to become spiritually rich, the last step was to come to this

town,

as he did, and sit in that center square and suffer the derision of others. Here was his great act of fraternal love. Could he love God so much that in order to love his neighbor perfectly he would be willing to give it all away, as he had, and then appear before them as a penniless pauper? And if anyone recognized him, all the better. For what a fall from grace, what an embarrassment, ah, see, this the lot of all politicians, at last, humbled, and good for him, good that what goes around, comes around. If, by that same and singular grace of God, he could withstand all this silent as a lamb before the shearer, God would grant him heaven and this

town

a reprieve.

And so it came to pass.

Wilkins got it done, he did it.

From the moment I saw that joy of facts on his face to a few hours ago when he died outside of

town,

the last part of his mission to head into the storm and try to convince any remnant stragglers to get back to safety, he did it. And he's happier than happy now, you would not believe what a complete and perfect happiness is now his, forever. And maybe you've been given something more, too, I don't know. Maybe you've received something a little like he did, a little lifting of the veil, a help to your flagging faith, maybe the first spark of a faith that never was, until now.

But let me tell you, none of you have any idea why things happen as they do. God's given you an extremely rare moment to have even a little of it explained, even if just a little, and it's true: blessed are those who haven't seen and yet believe. And not without reason did God once ask a man,

'Where were you when the foundations
of the world were laid?'

You, all of you here, all of all of you everywhere, everyone, you have no idea. You've heard that God works for the good of those who love him and it's true. But so many of you don't love God. And yet He loves all of you, so much, you have no idea. And I'm not just talking about 'look around, the sky, sunsets, God is an artist, God is love,' yes, all of that is true, but so many of you say it like a cliché, like you don't even believe it and moving on anyways. I'm saying God holds everything in perfect harmonious balance by his sovereign providential plan and yet never, not even for a second, violates our free will. Angels and men, us too. Isn't that so cool,' Seraphim says, taking a sip of the beer in his left hand and sip from the other mug too, 'so, amazing, it's hard for the angelic intellect to grasp it too, believe me, that perfect, spider-silk thin balance between He's always in total control and we're totally free and all He wants is for us to choose Him and love Him and in doing so we'll be choosing our best selves too, ha," another sip of beer, double mug, "there's a nice cliché for you, best-self, best version of yourself, but, sure, yeah it's all true. And none of you have any idea."

A man gets up in the assembly but Seraphim has already read his mind. He points at the man.

"Why," Seraphim says, asking rather. "Why did God allow this? How could God if God is good allow such evil? Why doesn't God prevent all evil, by the way. Why didn't God just stop the plague from spreading better yet from materializing in the first place?"

The man slumps back down in his chair.

"You do not understand anything," Seraphim says, "humanity. And it's beautiful. God looks on this with love. He made you with limitations, you're not supposed to understand all things and you only fall into trouble when you try to, try to grasp it all, get all of it, every ounce of meaning and purpose and just why, into your heads. But you can't. You weren't made to. And that really is so much of the problem here. You all trying to be something you're not meant to be and in fact do not possess the requisite material to be. You first deny God, deny a larger, universal plan, then deny smaller truths, all truths, and then somehow it is at that point that you believe you can, what with your science and formulas, understand it all. You have no idea how much that makes all of us laugh, us angels. Nothing is as funny as that. The human being who believes he is self-made and self-sufficient and capable of understanding everything."

"Understanding everything," Seraphim says, pausing to take another left then right drag on his beer. He's what they call a deep drinker. It looks like a normal swig, but after just one a quarter of the mug is drained. "Understand everything," he says again, "I tell you, and I know, we know from watching you, you hardly understand the most basic things. And when it comes to things more rudimentary than that, simpler than basic, treat others with respect, see God's Image and Likeness in all people, do unto others....well. So, anyways, like I was saying before, to answer your question, Mr. Young," pointing to the had stood up then slumped back down man. "God is in charge and allows things to happen because He is in charge. I know that sounds circular, but allow me to explain.

God gave people free will.

There is no love without free will.

God making us puppets and forcing us to love Him is not love and is no different than a man forcing a woman to marry him. Maybe she does love him, even under those circumstances, but he'll never know. God, who is Love, God is Love, as you all either know or have heard, cannot contradict Himself. He cannot do evil. To restrict the free will of his crowned creation would be evil. You would all be the bride walking to the altar deterministically led by fate, by tyranny, by everything except your own free will. What can you pathetic humans give to God? What can you hope to give God who is infinitely perfect in Himself, who needs nothing? One thing: your will. You can choose, freely, to say yes to Him, day after day unto eternity forever. And here, it's nothing but love. You, the bride, you chose Him, the Divine Spouse and that is love and nothing else is love. So, as you know, Adam and Eve told God no. God, always in charge, allowed man to abuse his free will, to say no, because that's love, just like I said, that's love, that's freedom. But Adam and Eve said no and so, okay, that great fall began this constantly falling world. So that's the beginning of an answer for you, Mr. Young. Bad things happen because you humans decided to choose the bad and you do choose the bad still. You want some, what, religious proof, that sin is real," Seraphim starts laughing, "right, I didn't think so. The most optimistic believers admit it's unfortunately true whereas the 98% rest of everyone, from the low burn pessimists to the midnight black-pilled nihilists, wallow in it.

People had a choice, they chose sin, and so they got the fallen world that comes with that—including its disease, its wars, its plagues, its death, its destruction. But before you protest again, this all-powerful God, what did He do in response? O happy fault, that merited for us, for you, such a Great Redeemer. Even the most bitter atheist would admit that if he believed this to be true, original sin, then God certainly had the right to obliterate mankind because they did the literal one thing He told them not to. But, no. God, who is Love, will not be outdone in goodness. That's your true answer, Mr. Young. It is that God always has a plan that is perfectly good until man, by misuse of his free will, thwarts it, leading to God responding by making the new plan better than before. Comply with God and things go swimmingly. But resisting Him will not lead to overcoming Him for His response will be something even better, your disobedience and infidelity responded to by love, providential care, goodness.

If you remember one thing before I get out of here let it be this: God cannot be outdone in goodness. His original plan for you is good. And His response to your failings is more goodness. He always brings about the good; good from good and good even out of bad, even out of what appears to be hopelessness.

Now, some things that seem bad, to you, are not. And some of these you do understand. The guy born into poverty who swears, later in life, he some kind of successful businessman, as you put it, that it was because of his poverty, not in spite of it, that he became a success. The Dominican baseball player, ah, yes, I became a major leaguer because of the horrible equipment and rock-strewn fields, using a milk carton for a glove, all that, and I bet that without this blessing that seems to many a disadvantage, I'd probably not have made it. With the quote en quote advantages of well-manicured fields, shiny new bats, shinier cleats and gloves, I'd probably had quit playing at age 12. Lesser thought of still are things like the guy with the scar or the mole or whatever on his face that made him self-conscious enough to be humble and pure. Without this "bad thing" he'd already have drowned in a pool of sin, of licentiousness, of broken hearts and lives and all kinds of diseases. But this one thing kept him in check and gave him the happy life, and the happy marriage, he has now. And another person just crippled by anxiety. And they can't stop worrying and just worry about all things, and all the time, and people pity them but it's precisely this "bad thing" that has made them a good hearted, empathetic person on the path to holiness. Without it, they'd have no fear of God, no respect for others, no respect for anything, and drunk on their own imagined power would long be lying destitute in some ditch somewhere. But you

understand nothing, that's what I'm saying.

Would it change your mind if I told you that this Dust Plague actually saved your country, at least for a few more decades? And maybe by then you'll have gotten it together. Saved your country because while many died because of it, and many of your cities lie in ruin, it's nothing compared to what would have happened without it. For, and I kid you not, seeing all this Dust Plague destruction has led a very important foreign leader who was about to lay complete, war-driven ruin to your country, to take compassion upon you.

I'm not a monster, am I?, he's asking himself
right now. *I could never now invade a country, not*
at this time of great need, those poor people.

And he's not going to invade. But he doesn't understand the providential hand here, no one does, expect you, in this room. Or what about the countless people who did die by way of the Dust Plague but are now in Heaven. Had they lived longer they would have fallen into grave sin, many of them, and no predestination here, not that they were meant for sin and perdition, you all know God desires all men to be saved, and amen, but, no, by their free choice, they would have fallen into sin. But they died not like that, not in sin. For them, for thousands of these people, yes, I can tell you, there were thousands,

salvation, in Christ, came in the
form of a Dust Plague.
But you don't understand any of this, and all
of life is like this, hidden, at times known to
God alone,

and we messengers, well, sometimes He allows us to let you all in on this Divine Comedy. I use this term in its classic sense. All of life is a comedy as in a happy ending: you're all meant for eternal, perfect bliss with God and He works so hard to help you, influencing you, prodding you, suggesting, dropping hints, to get you there. Some people need a little help.

Some people need to be killed in a
Dust Plague to avoid damnation.

But you understand nothing and as such perhaps this last story I'll leave you with will be most illustrative. You all know Mrs. Wilcox of the would be million dollar lawsuit and the broken eggs, the spilled milk. To her, my yelling and causing the event was just the straw on the camel's back, these homeless scum, and so on. But I saved her life. She dropped the groceries and returned to the Co-op and re-purchased them and then went home. Had her original path not been altered she would have been killed by a car crossing the street a little past us, in Philadelphia Court. No, it wasn't her time yet. She still has to do something for her future grandson who isn't born yet. Twenty-four years from now. Then she'll be free to go. You understand nothing, you see, least of all how much God really loves you and takes care of you, in every moment."

There is no murmuring amongst the assembly now, there is no sound, nothing, no one says anything and cannot help looking, maybe even staring at Seraphim, and everyone is kind of frozen like that. Seraphim begins to sing, an a capella version of *Adoro Te Devote* and while no one in this room knows this song, and only a few even know that Latin is the language he is singing in, it is strong evidence for his self-proclaimed angelic status. It is beautiful to a level simply not human in capacity, off a human scale, any scale, hereto known or even imagined. He finishes singing and disappears before them. The near empty beer mugs smash to the ground and then, slowly, recede into nothingness, disappearing not as fast, but all the same as he did. And that, one would have to admit, is pretty freaking cool. Nice exit, you'd have to say. The assembly keeps staring ahead, at the spot where he had been standing, speaking, singing. They don't even notice the sunlight pouring in through the glass panes, the glass wet from the rain but steadily being warmed by the sun, the sun emanating from a blue sky, a high, blue sky which, at present, does not contain even a single cloud.

Because it really is a most beautiful

town.

ABOUT THE AUTHOR

GRACJAN KRASZEWSKI is the author of four books: the novel *Thermonuclear Mirth* and the book of essays *The Hippo Lectures*—both from Arouca Press—along with the novel *The Holdout* and the Civil War history *Catholic Confederates.* Holder of a PhD in history (from Mississippi State University) he has taught, and teaches, at universities in the Pacific Northwest and Midwest. He played baseball in college, professionally in Europe in the Czech Republic and Belgium, and for the Polish National Team.

www.ingramcontent.com/pod-product-compliance
Lightning Source LLC
LaVergne TN
LVHW050134080526
838202LV00061B/6488